The Heart of the Spring Lives On

A Bennett Spring Novel

Book 2

Laura L. Valenti

Cover Photography by Bailey Reid

Publishing Coordinator – Sharon Kizziah-Holmes
Book Design – Monica L. Holcomb

Indie Pub Press
Springfield, Missouri

ISBN -13: 978-1-970560-11-4

DEDICATION

Dedicated to each and every one who has ever come into the valley of Brice and Bennett and the Osages' Sacred One and fallen in love, with a place, with a spirit, with the heart of Bennett Spring.

And with gratitude to God for the gift of this beautiful place, that many of us may visit and some have come to call their own sweet home.

AUTHOR'S PREFACE

It is with gratitude and joy that I write today, one year after its original publication that hundreds of copies of *The Heart of the Spring* have been sold here in Bennett Spring State Park, Lebanon and Laclede County, Missouri. More are now venturing out to other parts of the United States as visitors, far and wide, take copies home with them. Even more gratifying are the emails, letters and messages I have been privileged to receive from so many, saying how much they enjoyed that first Bennett Spring novel. There is no finer music to soothe a writer's soul than to know something you've penned has touched another's heart and brought a smile, a tear or a sweet memory to mind. As a result, I am pleased to offer this sequel, *The Heart of the Spring Lives On.*

This new story picks up eleven years after the first, as Ben Darling, Becky's little brother embarks on his own adventures as a grown man. All of the Darling family members are back and new friends come to add their part to the history of Bennett Spring during 1935 as the Civilian Conservation Corps, often known as the CCC, builds the structures that we all love at Bennett Spring State Park.

While the individuals, situations and conversations as related here are completely fictional, the CCC did labor at Bennett Spring. Here and at many other state parks across our nation during those lean years of the 1930s, the CCC saved families from starvation and ruin while building the most extensive park system the world has ever known. To me, history has always been a wondrous story book, just waiting to be explored and yet for reasons I will never understand it is at times reduced to a list of hard dry facts, leaving a bad aftertaste for those who do not share its adventure and romance. My purpose here is to once again remind one and all, myself included, that our history has been written by living, breathing men and women, who like us, struggle with circumstances that threaten to overwhelm. Their stories help us in our own challenging times to remember that with faith and love, we can triumph in the face of adversity.

Once again, I have to say, this is not my story, but rather one given to me by the good Lord to pass on, and for that I am most appreciative. I am also thankful to so many who have graciously lent their talents to make this book complete, including Ellen Gray Massey, well-known Ozark author and editor, for her tireless editing, encouragement and wise counsel; Debbie Blades, my ever-patient proofreader and dear friend for her hard work and research on my behalf; Eric Adams, Laclede County's own photographic wizard and one of his gifted students, Bailey Reid for yet another beautiful cover and their enthusiasm for this project; Jim and Carmen Rogers for generous material support; Diane Tucker, Bennett Spring Park Naturalist for her encouragement and willingness to share history and photos of Bennett Spring State Park; to Steve and Pam Bunch of Montreal,

Missouri and their Percherons, Cadet, Flame and Mark and especially to Steve for his assistance in ensuring the authenticity of part of this manuscript; to Susie Van Camp and other Hufstedler family members of Oregon County for sharing their history and friendship; and always to my husband, Warren and his patient support of my dream of writing novels and my children, Francesca and Jón, Lisa and Clayton, Ricardo and Tiffany, and Emmanuel and their children, Dante, Dominic, Austin, Cooper and Tyson, for their love, encouragement and support.

Like many others who now claim Bennett Spring as home, I came to this valley over 40 years ago, as a result of a career change, my husband's, with the Missouri Department of Conservation. Warren worked over 21 years as the assistant manager of the Bennett Spring Trout Hatchery during the 1980s and 1990s. As a result, we were blessed to live in the park our first eight years here and then moved to our own home a couple of miles up the road. We raised our children at Bennett Spring and I know wherever they go in this world, like me, they will always think of Bennett Spring fondly.

I sincerely hope this book will be received in the same spirit it was written, as an offering from one who loves Bennett Spirng and the folks who call it home, for a few years or a lifetime. Meanwhile, blending history and fiction is far from an exact science. While there are no confirmed cases of women working undercover in the CCC, there are over 200 known cases of women fighting during the

US Civil War, just seventy years earlier, masquerading as men. There are also hundreds of documented cases of surrogates serving as soldiers during that same war in place of those who could afford to pay for them to do so. Likewise, the CCC workers at Bennett Spring were actually older World War I veterans and not 20 year olds found at many CCC camps throughout the rest of the state and entire nation. Nonetheless, this author's imagination made a stretch, to bring a fictional story to life, employing many aspects of real periods of our country's history, difficult times for so many. To any who find this offensive in any way, I offer my apologies. To all the rest, like me, who simply love a good story with a historical basis, it is my prayer that you will enjoy reading *The Heart of the Spring Lives On* as much as I enjoyed writing it!

Laura L. Valenti, author

Bennett Spring, Missouri

Chapter 1

He was going to be late for dinner and he could already hear his father grumbling about it. He punched the accelerator, pushing his old Ford to pick up even more speed, racing downhill in the evening dusk. Every Thursday since moving to town earlier in the year, he had come home for supper. It was easier that way since Friday was his day off and he could stay over. If his luck held he might still make it. Then he heard them.

Half a dozen bluetick hounds burst from the underbrush and clambered across the dirt roadway in front of him. Ben Darling tromped on the brakes, locking up the back wheels on the thin gravel, sending his Ford Model A spinning nearly out of control. As the roadway divided at the state park entrance, he fought to keep from slamming into the fast approaching trees. He caught a glimpse of a scrawny man on a startled mule as the vehicle skidded by. Junior Kendrix was also struggling to regain control of his transportation as the animal kicked wildly at the sight of the careening automobile.

"Junior!" Ben employed a mule kick of his own to the car door as fast as his wheels found purchase on the roadside weeds. "Are you crazy?" Ben leapt out onto the road and started back towards the man in ragged overalls who had finally managed to calm the whirling mule.

"Good evening to you, Deputy Darling," Junior chuckled with a red face. "I have to admit. I do like the way that sounds. Deputy Darling. Flows real nice, don't it?"

"Well, never mind that." The deputy tried to sound stern, despite the circumstances. As the youngest member of the county sheriff's department, he still found coming across as authoritative to be a major challenge. Here on his home territory at Bennett Spring, it was even more of a struggle. "You 'bout got both of us kilt!" Ben hoped righteous indignation might carry him through.

"Now, Ben...er, Deputy," Junior stammered. "You know how it is. You can't control where them puppies run. Once they take off, you got to listen and do your best to catch up."

Junior leaned back as far as the laws of physics would allow while still astride his mule and squinted at Ben. "Does that uniform make you look taller? I swear, Deputy, you are taller than when I last saw you!"

"Sure, Junior," Ben replied with more than a touch

of skepticism. "You've known me all your life and it's just now dawned on you I'm not twelve years old anymore!"

The man on the mule snickered with a near toothless smile. "Well, maybe that's so. I do still tend to think of you as—whoa! Listen for it! There it is! Them puppies have got something!"

Junior's eyes brightened as the distant warbling of the dogs had indeed changed, indicating they had treed their quarry. "Sorry about the mishap, but you seem to be none the worse for it. Those dogs are a-callin'. Got to go, son. We'll talk another day!" He laid a switch in a gentler fashion than not to the mule's backside and jauntily set off across the road, following the dogs' excited calls.

Ben shook his head with a grin in spite of the momentary aggravation. It was good to be home. He drove the short distance from what was now the park's official entrance, past the exquisite ever-flowing waters of Bennett Spring. If he wasn't already late to his mother's dinner table, he would have gladly stopped to enjoy the blue-green spring's calming influence. It was nearly impossible to describe and yet it was something he had missed desperately since moving to Lebanon, over ten miles away. Instead, he glanced longingly at the deep beautiful waters of the great spring as he drove past slowly and let his thoughts drift back to days gone by.

"Benji!" His little sister, Esther, squealed the family nickname and ran to give him a hug as he opened the front door to his parents' home. His own home, no matter where he lived, he thought with a smile. He returned a quick embrace of his own.

"How are you, Sprig?"

"Good to see you, Benji." His older sister, Becky, looked up from where she was setting the table. Hannah, their mother, tended to steaming pots on the hot wood stove and Zeb Darling, seated in the far corner of the room, peered around the side of his newspaper long enough to mutter, "It's about time."

"I know, I know," Ben tried to explain. "I'm sorry. I got a late start and then I nearly collided with a couple of Junior Kendrix's best coon dogs, coming down the hill tonight. I swear, he's a menace to other folks sometimes."

"You act like that's something new," Zeb Darling retorted as he tossed the newspaper aside. "It's been that way ever since he took over for his older brother, Buster, when he got hisself shot. It's what finally landed your brother in jail—"

"Ma, are we nearly ready?" Becky interrupted, narrowing her eyes in her brother's direction as a clear warning.

"Yes, are we ready to eat yet, Hannah? We're getting pretty hungry here." Zeb allowed his attention to be easily diverted.

"Sorry," Ben mouthed silently in Becky's direction with more than a hint of mischief on his face.

"I daresay you are," his wife answered with a glance in Zeb's direction. She pulled a pan of golden brown biscuits from the oven and continued,

"But then you are always hungry. I think you must have been born with a tapeworm, Zeb. I can't imagine any other way you could eat as much as you do and still stay so skinny!"

"I ain't skinny." He feigned insult with a grin and patted Becky's protruding belly as he smiled broadly. "I just work hard to keep my girlish figure, unlike some folks I know."

"Well, I know about the working hard part." Becky let out an exaggerated pant that puffed the lock of blond hair which swept across her forehead. She dropped wearily into a chair at the table as she waited for her mother to finish at the stove.

"I know you do," her mother added. "The last part is the hardest, but it won't be long now and you and J.C. will have your own baby to hold. And after all these years, it's high time."

"Oh, I didn't tell you! Miz Darcey is telling me I need to go see Dr. McComb in Lebanon. She thinks…" She hesitated and looked around as if she was afraid to say her next words aloud. "She thinks I may be carrying twins! I didn't know whether to laugh or cry when she told me! She says she can't be sure but she thinks it's real likely, so I'm going to see the doctor sometime next week."

"Oh, Becky." Her mother nearly dropped the basket of biscuits. "If that's what the midwife says…What will you do?"

"Ma, it's all right, really," Becky laughed. "We'll be fine. I mean, you will lend me Esther once in awhile to help out, won't you?" She smiled at her little sister who wriggled with excitement.

In short order, a hot meal of chicken and dumplings, home canned green beans, cinnamon-laced applesauce and hot biscuits graced their table.

With heads bowed, the family grasped hands and Zebulon Darling's deep baritone echoed in the silence. "Lord, for what we about to receive, make us truly grateful," he ended the blessing. "In the name of your Son, Our Savior, we pray. Amen."

Zeb served the main dish from a steaming pot in front of him and passed the remainder of the items around the table as the conversation ricocheted from one to another.

"So, two for the price of one, hey, Sis?" Ben returned to the topic at hand. "You and J.C. have waited all these years and now you're not wasting any more time, are you?"

"Well, it's not like we planned any of this," she sighed. "I've been busy helping Miz Darcey deliver babies all around the valley for years. She tells me she's ready for me to do most all of them, but that's not going to happen any time soon now. But for all those deliveries, it's about broke my heart a few times that J.C. and I couldn't make it happen in our own house. But now if God has seen fit to send us two at once, I'm certainly not going to complain!"

Her brother grinned at his sister's obvious happiness. "So, things going all right for J.C. at the newspaper?"

"Oh, yes. He fusses with this one and that but that's

just the nature of the business. He loves it all, being editor, you know. It has lots of headaches and pressure that I wouldn't want." She laughed and added, "But then he says he can't imagine delivering babies either! I guess the good Lord has work that is made special for each of us."

"And the new book?"

"Oh, he got a letter from the New York publishers last week. They say it will be out in about another six months, a book all about life here in Brice and around Bennett Spring. Can you imagine?"

Ben chuckled. "No, honestly, I can't, but I guess folks in New York or Chicago can't imagine what it's really like here so if J.C. can tell 'em and they'll buy his book to find out, that ain't a bad thing. He must be pretty happy about now. New babies and a new book both on the way."

"Oh, he is. He works too many hours but other than that, he's doing fine. So what's the news from town? Do you still like your job?"

"Oh, it's interesting. There's no doubt about that." Ben answered the second question first, as he shoveled heaping spoonfuls of beans and applesauce onto his plate. "Lots to learn, that's for sure. Some of it is the kind of thing you can study up on, like the paperwork for booking a prisoner and the serving of warrants, but a lot of it is like Sheriff Sam says, you just got to watch it, work it and pray you live through it!"

"Well, that's encouraging." His mother peered at him uncertainly. "I mean, that he thinks you will live through it. Let's hope so! What with the likes of these bank robbers running around the countryside, it's not just idle chatter these days. I know Bonnie Parker and Clyde Barrow are gone now but there are plenty of others out there who think they can take their place. I worry that they will try to make their big reputation in the little towns like Lebanon. I can't help but think you could find an easier, safer way to make a living, Benji." Hannah brought up what was obviously an old argument.

"Well, I probably could," he sighed and gave her a wink. "But not near as interesting, Ma, that's for sure. I'm not cut out to be no doctor or lawyer or such. And I'm not the kind to do like Pa either, the same thing, day in and day out. Not saying nothing bad about you delivering the mail, sir, you know that. I'm glad somebody does it but it's just not for me." Benji hurried on to explain himself completely before offending his father. "For now, anyway, I feel like this work is good for me."

"Any work is good for you or anybody else right now," Zeb added flatly as he sipped the warm broth from his plate of dumplings. "Hannah, don't take on so. The boy's got a job and that's more than a great many can say right now. Don't be complaining about anybody doing honest labor. There's plenty who aren't working at all and way too many who are doing the other kind. This whole world being without is part of what's caused all these bank robbers to spring up in the first place. I'm glad our son is on the right side of things, at least. There are those who have to worry about theirs becoming the next Clyde Barrow!"

She sighed in exasperation. "You're right. I'm sorry, Benji. Thanks be to God that you have a job at all and especially work that you enjoy. I look at those poor boys working down in the valley at the Civilian Conservation Corps camp every time I walk by and I know their mamas must be missing them something fierce. So far from home...." Her voice drifted away.

"That is true," Becky nodded in agreement. "It's bad enough having J.C. stay over a night or two each week in town when the presses don't run 'til late or they have an extra big issue at the paper, but I can't imagine having my husband or even my brother so far away like that." She stood up and headed for the glass jar sitting next to the pump handle at the sink. "Does anyone else want more milk?"

"Yes, please." Pig-tailed Esther held up her empty glass while turning back to her brother. "I think it's exciting that you're a deputy sheriff! Do you get to wear your gun all the time?"

"Just when I'm working, Sprig. That's all," he added with a small smile. Why was it the first thing the kids always wanted to know about was the gun?

"Which is why it's hanging on the pegs by the door," her mother added sharply. "Nobody's working as a deputy here tonight."

"It's not really my gun yet," Ben added. "Sheriff Sam was good enough to lend me this one and I'm buying it a little at a time out of each pay check. Deputies have to bring their own gun to the job."

"Gosh, I didn't know that," Esther continued. "I like the new gold star on your car door. Does that mean you're driving an official sheriff's car now?" Esther hurried on, eyeing her mother carefully.

Ben laughed out loud and quickly covered his mouth with the back of his hand. "Yes and no, I suppose. It's still my car but it gets used for official purposes now. Sheriff Sam says if they have the money, they'll pay me some for my gas when they can and in the meantime, I'm considered on patrol whenever I'm driving around."

"Pretty tricky way for the county to get free labor and transport out of the deal," Zeb grumbled under his breath.

"Maybe so," Ben answered, "but I've got no complaints."

"Well, I'm glad for you," Becky grinned and kicked him gently beneath the table. "J.C. says the lucky man who finds a job that matches his personality will never work a day in his life. I guess he would know," she chuckled softly.

"I'd say that'd be true on both counts," Ben agreed. "So what are those CCC boys doing of late, Pa?"

"Hmph! Wasting a lot of government money, if you ask me." Zeb waved his knife as he spread home-churned butter on a hot biscuit. "I mean, all that they're building down there in the valley is real practical or purty, don't get me wrong. I suppose as they keep making this into a real park, they're going to need it all as more people come. But it seems to me President Roosevelt could've done it a lot cheaper, hiring local boys and not paying them boys' room and board what with 'em building their own barracks down there. You know what I'm talking about. What are they going to do with all that when they go?" He stopped speaking for a moment as if he expected an answer but none of his children offered one. They had heard this one-sided argument before.

"You know," he continued as he loaded blackberry jam on the same biscuit. "They've been here a couple of years already and they say they're scheduled to stay a couple more but any way you go at it, they ain't going to be here forever. Sooner or later, they've got to go and then what? I mean, these CCC boys are building stuff all over the country and I suppose it's one of President Roosevelt's answers to all of this economic depression they keep talking about but—"

"Well, I'm sure somebody's got that figured out," Ben offered tentatively. "I know the sheriff was talking to Captain Smith and they're bringing in some new replacements next week. He said they'd lost enough in the last couple of months that they had to bring in some others to fill in."

"How did they lose 'em?" Esther looked up with a frown.

"Well, they're not really lost. It just means they had to leave the Civilian Conservation Corps. Let's see. I think he said one got pneumonia, another broke his arm and another left to get married. It just means for one reason or another, they've left and they ain't coming back."

"Aren't coming back," his mother corrected softly. "For heaven sakes, Benji, we're trying to teach the child the King's English."

"Oh." He ducked his head in obedience to his mother's request. "They aren't coming back so they had to get some other boys in here to take their place, you see? They got a crew to work and a certain amount of work to get done. If they don't have enough men, they'll get behind and then..." he hesitated for only a moment, "they might be here forever!"

"Smart aleck!" His father grinned in spite of himself.

"Well, I don't care if they are," Esther said. "I like 'em."

"That's all fine and good." Her mother reached over to flip the child's napkin at her, indicating it belonged in her lap and not crumpled up on the table. "You stay away from those CCC boys and their barracks. You don't have any business over there."

"Oh, Ma, we weren't doing nothing. Me and Alice was taking the butter down to the hotel and some of them—"

"Esther, Esther. We weren't doing anything. Alice and I were. Good grief, what do they teach over there in that school anyway?"

"Reading, writing, 'rithmetic and how to put a worm down a girl's back, just like when I was in school," Ben sniggered while glancing at Becky.

"Well, obviously grammar isn't part of their regular lessons." His mother shook her head in resignation.

"Anyway," Esther continued. "Did you know some of them are from as far away as Detroit?"

"Really?" Ben seemed surprised.

"One feller that Alice was talking to said he was born in New York. That's a really long way from here, huh, Pa?"

"Yes, Esther," Zeb answered. "Detroit and New York are both a 'fur' piece from here."

"'Fur' enough that you need to be staying away from them." Her mother repeated her admonition. "A men's camp like that is no place for young girls. I hear of you down there again, they'll be a switchin' in your future. Do we understand each other, young lady?" She stood and began to clear the dinner dishes.

"Yes ma'am." The eleven year old looked down at her empty plate as her lower lip slid forward.

"I don't hold anything against any of them individually," Hannah added. "I wouldn't even mind having one or two to dinner sometime as a way of helping out."

"Now, how you going to do that, Ma?" Ben chuckled. "You can't exactly go through a-pickin' and a-choosin' who to invite."

"Oh, you know your mother," Zeb grumbled with a smile on his face. "She'd invite the whole camp up here if she could figure out a way to feed them all at once."

"Be not forgetful to entertain strangers, for thereby some have entertained angels unawares," Hannah quoted from the Book of Hebrews and wagged a finger in her husband's direction.

Ben and Becky shared a smile as once again, like so many genteel disputes over the years between their parents, this one ended with a scripture quote from Hannah.

"Hey, Sprig," Benji caught his little sister's attention. "What kind of cake did I see over there on the table by the stove?"

"Oh, Ma's ginger cake with white icing!" Her eyes shone as her banishment from the forbidden CCC camp was momentarily forgotten.

While Hannah washed dishes at the sink, pumping water into the metal sink basin, Becky sat at the table and worked on flour sack embroidered blocks for a baby quilt. "I've been working on a quilt as well as a knitted afghan for one and now I may need to be doubling up," she laughed as she added colorful stitches to form lambs, chicks and bunnies. Zeb returned to his newspaper while Esther labored over her school books at the opposite end of the table from her older sister.

"From what I see here," Zeb snapped his paper, "J.C. is giving them boys in Washington, D.C. notice they best be paying attention to what that ol' boy over there in charge of Germany is doing now, re-arming what used to be the Kaiser's troops. We had to go over there and straighten out the mess for England and all of Europe once before because they didn't pay attention to what those Germans were doing until it was too late. J.C.'s right in his editorial here. There's no need to be doing that again."

"Oh, Pa, that was yesterday's editorial. Heaven knows what's in today's edition, since you get it a day late in the mail. Now you're even beginning to sound like J.C." Becky heaved a sigh. "All that politics and such."

"Politics and such is what keeps the world goin' round, young lady. Don't you ever forget it! If'n some of those boys in New York and Washington would pay a little more attention in the first place and not be so interested in just lining their own pockets, we wouldn't be having the problems that we're having in this country right now. It's 1935, for crying out loud, and do you realize…."

Zeb's tirade went on but Ben Darling let the words roll by. He leaned back against the wall. How many evenings had he spent in this very room? And how many of those, when he was much younger, had he only thought about how he couldn't wait to leave? Now as he thought of returning to his rented room in town tomorrow evening, where he slept alone, all he could think was he couldn't wait until he had his own little house, his own family. But how was that going to happen when he didn't know a single girl he'd even care to ask out, let alone settle down with? Slow down, boy, he cautioned himself. One thing at a time. Still, the loneliness that waited only a day away could not be denied.

"Don't be dawdling there, Miss," Hannah's voice cut through his silent musings. "There's still cream to be churned into butter tonight. Miz Laraine will be looking for it at the hotel tomorrow." She poured the rich liquid into the clear glass butter churn as she spoke.

A heavy sigh escaped Esther as she turned back to her school work.

"Let me have it, Ma." Ben turned to straddle the bench and plunked the gallon jar down between his knees.

He spun the handle to turn the paddle of the butter churn as they continued to visit. The activity he had once considered unbearably monotonous brought back even more memories.

"Did I tell you I saw Miz Josie up town the other day?" Ben continued. "She's running a boarding house in Lebanon with her niece, and I even ate dinner there one night with another deputy. When I saw her last week, she said she still misses Bennett Spring and she misses you, Becky. She says working with her niece is all right but that you were the best worker she ever had!"

Becky shook her head with a broad smile at the compliment. "I tried to tell her when she sold the Brice Inn that she would miss this valley," Becky replied. "She said she wanted to work as a clerk in a store. I guess she thought that would be less of a work-all-the-time job rather than running an inn. And now she's running a boarding house in town?" She snorted. "Same thing, different location."

Ben chuckled. "That's exactly what she said. She worked in a shop for a little while but she didn't have much interest in the ladies' hats and shoes and such so she ended up back in what she does best, work or no work."

He churned for a few moments in silence before he asked another question. "Speaking of other folks, Ma, how's Grampy Trundle doing these days? I haven't heard much about him since Grammy's funeral last fall."

"There's not been a lot to tell really," Hannah answered. "Zeb checks on him more often than ever on his mail route. I send milk up there once a week with Esther and she always brings an empty jar back from him, but I don't know. It's hard with an old one like that, especially once their mate goes. Zeb, how is he?"

"Oh, he's all right, all things considered. Even before Grammy died, he'd got to the point where he didn't do a lot. Still plants the big garden and he's got him quite a start on that already this spring so that's a good sign. Grammy told me last year they don't get much of a check these days from their son in Texas. I imagine like a lot of folks he hasn't got anything spare to send. Still, the church folks keep him supplied with a little here and a little there. I try to find out if he's doing all right with food and such but you know, he don't say much."

Ben nodded as he listened to the news about the man that had been an adopted grandfather to them all. He would have to make time himself to get up to that cabin, deep in the woods, for a little visit. The butter finally began to form as Esther finished her homework.

"You're lucky that your brother stuck around to save you tonight," Hannah admonished her youngest. "Another small piece of cake if you like and then it's time for you to be getting up to bed."

"Ah, Ma," she began to protest, but the effort was short-lived.

"There's nothing to be fussing about, Miss Priss," Zeb Darling cut in.

Becky winced as she recognized the less-than-favorite pet name her father had often used on her in years past when she was about to get into trouble.

"Yes, sir," the little one answered, despite her dragging steps. After eating her last piece of cake in slow motion, she kissed and hugged each one good night before climbing the ladder to her loft bedroom. "You sleeping across the way, Benji?"

"Yes, I am, so you settle down quick and don't be having no rowdy parties up there with your teddy bears, you hear? Otherwise, I know I won't get any sleep at all!"

"Oh, Benji," she grinned broadly at his teasing. "I'll see you in the morning then."

"Yes, ma'am. Bright and early to milk cows, slop hogs, fetch eggs, all kinds of big stuff."

"Oh, Benji," she repeated as she climbed the ladder with a giggle.

His mother smiled. "Thank you, Benji, for being such a good brother." She patted his shoulder as she walked by.

"Hey, it's not easy being the youngest," he added. "I remember it well."

"Being the youngest or losing that spot?" his father asked.

"Both, I guess," he smiled, "but by the time, Esther came along, I didn't mind giving it up. I just remember sometimes feeling like you're not only the littlest person in the outfit but the littlest person ever."

"Really?" Becky stopped stitching and looked up. "I never knew that."

"Well, it's not a big thing really," he glanced down in mild embarrassment. "It's just, well, you get lonesome, that's all."

"You still get lonely, don't you?" Becky could always see right through him, he remembered too late.

"Well, yeah, I guess so," he shrugged and stood up in search of a second piece of cake and a cup of coffee. Anything to focus the attention elsewhere.

"You need to find yourself a good woman and settle down," his mother commented, as she patted the churned butter into a round and wrapped it in a square of cheese cloth. "Have you seen the Turner girl again, now that you're living in town?"

"Lila Turner?" He shook his head and looked down with a cock-eyed grin. His mother was ever the matchmaker.

"Well, Benji, now how can you expect to settle down if you don't find yourself a proper young lady—"

"Ma, I'll find me a girl, one of these days," he laughed, "but for now, I've got plenty to keep me busy. Besides, Lila Turner is off to Springfield or Rolla or the like with them college boys. She doesn't have any interest in a country boy from Brice—"

"Now, don't be selling yourself short," his mother protested.

"Hannah, let the boy be," Zeb stepped in. "He ain't going to get married no sooner for you fussing at him."

"Well, I never thought much of Lila Turner anyway." Becky sniffed as she began to pack up her quilting materials. "Pretty snooty girl, if you ask me."

"Oh, she's all right," Ben added, "but not exactly my type."

"And what is your type, young man?" his mother asked.

"Well, I dunno," he shrugged, as his ears began to turn red and the color spread to his cheeks. "Somebody nice, but who knows how to do stuff. I don't really know what to say around those girls who only talk about clothes and hats and shoes or who's going to what party. I mean, if a girl don't know how to fish and cook and hike or do something else interesting, what's the point?"

Becky and Hannah burst into simultaneous laughter and Ben's face turned almost purple. "Well, you know what I mean!" he blurted out, too late, in his own defense.

Zeb Darling eyed all three of them and then offered his son a way out. "Benji, do you mind to drive your sister home tonight? She walked over here this afternoon, which I understand she says is good for her, but walking home in the dark is another thing. You said J.C. was staying in town tonight, didn't you?" He raised an eyebrow in Becky's direction.

"Yes. They've just started printing a small once-a-week paper for Marshfield and he was going to stay and make sure they get it out on time," Becky sighed. "He'll be home tomorrow."

"Sure, Sis, I'll take you home." Ben leapt at the chance to turn the conversation away from his love life, or lack of it. "Let me go out and and clean out the front of my car." He was out the door before more could be said.

Zeb seized his opportunity once his son was gone. "You know, you two are to blame for the reason that boy is going to have trouble finding a wife."

Both women stopped what they were doing to stare at him. "What in heaven's name are you talking about, Zeb Darling?" his wife began. "Nobody wants that boy settled more—"

"It ain't about the wanting, Hannah," Zeb continued as he folded up his newspaper. "The problem is, look at the two of you and what some poor girl has got to measure up to. No matter how you figure it, that's not going to be easy to find!"

CHAPTER 2

Jessica shivered in her thin flannel gown as she stood staring out the window at another cold gray dawn. She could see the Eleven Point River in the distance. She had waited forever for the end to another long Ozarks winter and now all it could do was rain. The weather matched her mood. Her twin brother, Jesse, was leaving to join the Civilian Conservation Corps soon. He was so excited about the opportunity, the chance to earn some real money for the family. She and Grammy, her little brother, Gabriel, and their baby sister, Grace would be on their own once he was gone, a prospect that terrified her.

She stripped off her gown and pulled on her dungarees. She hesitated in front of the cracked wavering mirror above the aged dresser, stretching, raising her arms above her head. Her ribs were plain to see, more easily than any time since she was ten years old. She shook her dark brown curls as she wriggled into a worn undershirt and then pulled on one of her father's oversized work shirts. The shabby softness of the old shirt brought back the comfort and smell of his embrace. It allowed her to pretend that he wasn't really gone forever and to remember better days before he went away. And now Jesse was leaving too. She took one last look in the mirror, her gaze stopping to rest on her own bright blue-green eyes. Her dad said they were the same color as a crystal clear Ozark spring. No crying today, she told herself as she turned away.

Why didn't she ever get to go, she wondered as she did up her boots with an angry tug at the laces. Why did she have to stay home with the babies and do laundry, always more laundry? Wasn't she the same age as Jesse? And yet he was leaving and she wasn't. And what if, like her father, he never came back? A different sort of chill swept over her at the thought and she scooted down the stairs to the warmth of the fire that Grammy already had going in the stove.

In spite of her mood, a small smile tugged at her heart at the sight of red-headed Grace, busy dressing behind the living room stove. She had done the same when she was little but now, as a grown woman, she gritted her teeth and dressed quickly in the unheated upstairs bedroom. It was late spring, but the weather still felt like winter.

"'Morning, Jessica," her little sister sang out as she walked past.

"Hey, Little Bit, how are you doing?"

"I'm doing fine," she answered from her comfy hideout behind the pot-bellied cast iron stove.

"'Mornin'," she greeted her grandmother who was shuffling about the kitchen. "Where's the boys?"

"Outside. I imagine Jesse is tellin' Gabe what'll need to be took care of once he's gone," Grammy answered while stirring a boiling pot of oatmeal.

Jessica frowned while she poured herself a cup of thin coffee. "Can't believe he's leaving," she muttered more to herself than to anyone else.

"I know it will be sad to see him go, but it's got to be done, Jessica. I'm trying real hard not to say nothin' to him to make it any worse. You know he don't really want to go but he knows..." Her grandmother leaned over the boiling pot to take a closer look.

"Knows? Knows what?" Jessica clenched her teeth in anger. "Does he know how hard it is to stay here? To be the one that never leaves? Does he know what it is to wash clothes until your fingers bleed?"

"Girl, what's wrong with you?" Grammy clapped the lid on the pot and shoved it to the cooler side of the stove. The old woman caught the girl off guard as she reached out with a bone-hard hand to grab a handful of young shoulder. "Don't you be adding to that boy's burdens, you hear? Hasn't he got enough to deal with? Sounds to me like somebody's feeling more than a might sorry for herself." She snorted. "If'n your fingers hurt, you best be rubbing some of that lard on 'em at night before you go to bed."

"Grammy, that is so nasty," Jessica sighed.

"Well, that may be but it works." Her grandmother chuckled and caught her granddaughter in a rough embrace. "I know this ain't the life a young girl dreams of," she whispered and tucked a wisp of dark hair behind Jessica's ear. "Ain't exactly the life I dreamed of neither, caring for two little ones in my old age, but we got to do what we got to do, darlin'. My sister Hazel keeps writing from California, telling me to come out there but it just ain't meant to be right now. Heaven knows, there ain't much left here of what there once was but your daddy loved you and he went off to do what he thought would save us. It didn't work out the way he planned is all."

With that, the tears Jessica had been holding back all morning broke loose. She didn't mean to cry, especially not where Grammy could see, but once Papa was mentioned, there was no stopping it.

"Now, I seen that a-comin'." Grammy gave her a pat and turned her loose. "I loved my son like no other but the consumption took him and he's gone. I do appreciate that you and Jesse went to bring him home and not leave him up there in Yankee country to be buried by strangers." She pulled a stack of metal bowls out of the upper cupboard with a clatter.

Jessica remembered the thrill of the train ride all the way to St. Louis. The people at the tuberculosis sanitarium had been very kind as was the tug boat captain where Papa had worked before he got so sick. If the trip had not been for such a terrible purpose—to bring her father's body home—it would have been great fun. The adventure of watching the scenery fly past the speeding train's windows waned in comparison to the sheer excitement, near panic at times, of making their way around the streets of the city. Riding on the streetcar with all those sparks shooting from the wires overhead was electrifying and the sight of the Mississippi River took her breath away. She was thrilled to be there but also so very glad she wasn't alone. And after only two days when all arrangements had been made and it was time to come home, she was happy about that as well.

"Here." Grammy handed her a tiny square jar. "It's lard mixed with essence of lilacs and some other herbs. It ain't no fancy hand lotion but it's the best of my mixin' and it will make your hands feel better. And Jessica…." The old woman took a deep breath and cupped her hands around her granddaughter's as she held the jar. "Your time will come—to go and find your own life. And when it does, you grab it with both hands and hang on tight! Until then, you're stuck here with me and these little ones a bit longer, is all. Like me, you just have to keep praying."

Jessica looked down and her tears welled up again, in shame this time. As old as Grammy was—and she would never tell, no matter how often she and Jesse had asked when they were younger—she never despaired and after all she'd suffered in her life, Jessica considered that quite an achievement.

"I know all that laundry is back-breaking but we

ought to be thankful for it," Grammy continued. "It brings in a little money and for now, we got to pray that's enough to get us by." And with that, she launched into one of her many stories about when she was a little girl and how hard life was after the war, the Civil War. Jessica tried to listen politely but her mind wandered. She dipped a spoonful of sorghum molasses from the jar on the table to put in her coffee. She didn't like it much but it was better than drinking it black and it was cheaper than sugar. As Grammy said, every penny had to count double nowadays.

Grace came into the kitchen and Jessica helped her up into a chair when she looked down at the little one's nearly worn out shoes. "Grace, you've got your shoes on the wrong feet again." Her big sister smiled. "Here, I'll switch them for you."

"I do it! I do it!" The child insisted.

"All right." Jessica pushed her gently up to the table. "After you eat then." She doled out a steaming bowl of oatmeal and stirred in some of the molasses and a little cold water. She missed the milk they used to enjoy, from their own cow and then later, purchased from the neighbors after they sold the cow. Now there was no money for either.

"I'll go find Jesse and Gabe," she called back over her shoulder. She threw a jacket over her shoulders and stepped outside. She could hear the river as it broke over the dam down around the bend, a short distance from the house and the tiny town of Riverton, on the Eleven Point River.

Once outside, she took a deep breath of the cool crisp air. Where would Jesse be going? she wondered again. Would he be close to another river somewhere? She contemplated life in a dry place with no running water and it wasn't a pleasant thought.

"Jesse! Gabe!" she called. "Breakfast!"

She took a peek in the chicken house and scooped up the three eggs she found there in the laying boxes and put them in the basket hanging by the door. She'd come back later to see if there were more.

The boys beat her to the back door of the house.

"Where you two been?" she asked as they all trooped inside.

"Just down to the river, Sis," her youngest brother, Gabe, answered for both of them as he sauntered ahead of her. "Having a talk, a man talk." He looked so much like a miniature version of Jesse, trying so hard to walk just like his older brother, it made her want to laugh out loud.

"Oh, a man talk," she repeated with a smile and rolled her eyes at Jesse, glancing sideways at the eight year old. "Well, I don't guess I need any part of that."

The gentle banter between the siblings continued through breakfast, interrupted by a knock at the front door.

Lyle Kravitz. "Lyin' Lyle", they called him in school, was the first thing Jessica thought when she saw him standing on the porch, but her brother was in a more generous frame of mind.

"I don't have a wagon no more," Jessica heard him tell Lyle. "You know that."

"No, but you can get old man Hufstedler down there at the mercantile to lend you his, the one your pa sold to him before he left. It used to be yours and you can handle them horses," Lyle whined.

Jessica began to listen in earnest once her beloved Max and Molly came into the conversation. The last thing her father had done before leaving was to sell them, their last pair of Percherons, as well as their last wagon to Hufstedler's Store. He said the money would see them through until he could find work. The truth is they could no longer afford to feed the horses and Jessica knew it. Still, it broke her heart to see them go. Mr. Hufstedler had been kind enough to tell her to come and visit them anytime she wanted.

Somehow, Lyle convinced Jesse to join him but her brother agreed only if Jessica came along as well.

"I'm leaving in a few days but we can help you out this once. What are you hauling?"

And that's how they ended up on a deserted road, halfway between Riverton and West Plains, looking over what was supposed to be an easy load of timber. Easy load, indeed. Nothing was ever easy with Lyle and the weather wasn't cooperating either. The darkening sky, the strengthening wind, it was a day to stay home, close to a hot fire, instead of out in the worsening weather.

Jesse and Lyle scrambled to load the big logs into the wagon while Jessica stood with the horses as they stamped and snorted uneasily in the growing gloom. Despite the fact that the job was not as easy as Lyle had promised, the boys still had the wagon loaded in short order. It was plenty full, making Jessica wish they had taken the time to add the high sideboards but Lyle had said there was no need. Jessica suspected he simply didn't want to take the time.

She could tell the horses had not been worked in awhile. Mr. Hufstedler was kind to them and she was thankful for that. Still, he was busy with his stores in Riverton and West Plains and he didn't have the time to take them out and work them the way they needed, on a regular basis. The wagon was a mess, covered in cobwebs and littered with acorns stored by mice or squirrels, but fortunately, Mr. Hufstedler had been willing to lend the animals and the rig when Jesse explained the situation. She tried not to think about it all as she rubbed the muzzles of what she considered to be her neglected darlings. Max and Molly stood nearly 18 hands high, almost six foot tall at the withers, the last of her grandfather's once prosperous hauling company, a victim of hard times as well as a changing world that had moved on from horses to trucks and tractors.

Now Lyle wanted to go back for one last big log. He said he had a good buyer for the wood, a builder, and he did not want to lose the chance to sell all he could. Jessica watched the two of them in a peek-a-boo fashion while maintaining her grip on the dancing draft horses as the thunder rumbled ever closer.

The sudden crack of lightning above their heads riveted Jessica's attention and terrified the already distressed horses. As they reared upwards, they pushed the wagon backwards, dropping the back wheels off the edge of the road. The load of logs shifted sideways and then broke loose. Jessica screamed a warning but it was too late. Sparks showered down from the lightning-struck tree top. She saw her brother's back, Lyle's fleeing figure, as he dropped his end of the log and dove sideways, and all those rolling logs crashing back down the hillside through the underbrush.

Smoke from the smoldering bough wafted overhead as Jessica brought the near hysterical horses under control and eased the wagon back onto the roadway. She jumped from the wagon and tied the horses' leads tightly to a nearby tree to make certain they didn't bolt again in their still agitated state.

"Jesse! Lyle! Jesse!" After all the noise of the last few moments, the woods were now eerily silent. The logs lay scattered in a haphazard zigzag pattern across the landscape. She heard a moan and caught a glimpse of a movement far to her right as someone rolled over in the dead leaves.

"Lyle!" Jessica scrambled towards him and then she saw her brother's crumpled gray coat further down the hill to the left. "Oh, Jesse..." she gasped through her tears.

It felt like hours, the time it took for her and Lyle to extricate her brother, get him into the wagon and make the drive back to town. She wanted so badly to cradle him against the bumps along the way, but she drove instead, slapping the lines on their rumps, pushing the horses to the limit, whatever it took to save her brother. She barked instructions to Lyle as to exactly how to support Jesse and she made it clear that to fail to do so would be more hazardous to his health than a loosed wagonload of timber.

Jessica didn't leave her twin brother's bedside for the next three days. She prayed with all that was in her for him to wake up again. She wasn't the only one who was worried. Of course, Grammy had the doctor come immediately but then he came again and even a third time. Jessica couldn't imagine how they would ever pay him but that was far down the list of her current worries. Her brother had a big lump on his head, two black eyes, bruises all over, and most unfortunately, a broken left leg. And once he did finally come back to them, she couldn't hush him up.

As fast as Grammy and the doctor left the room, Jesse started laying out his plan to her. It was as if he had done nothing but scheme the whole of those days he appeared to be only sleeping.

"Look," he began, his voice keen with excitement. "I know it sounds scary but you can do this. I know you can. Jessica, I've got to keep my place in the CCC. President Roosevelt's not going to be paying for this kind of work forever. You know we've been waiting for months for all the paperwork and such for me to get a place and now we can't afford to lose it. We need that money now. You've seen how thin Gabe and Grace are getting. There's no money for shoes or medicine for Grammy and the little ones or even basic groceries anymore. And I know you go to bed hungry plenty of nights, too. Don't tell me you don't."

She shook her head in defiance. "All right, I won't but Jesse, this is crazy!" she sputtered. "I couldn't!"

"There's something more, Jessica. I've not said anything before. Grammy knows but…"

"But what?"

"Papa took out a note with the bank against the house before he went to St. Louis. If we don't pay and soon, they'll take the house. I didn't say anything before because I figured with the CCC money we could manage, but now…"

"Oh my stars, Jesse! The house?"

"It's all we got left and I'm sorry but I don't know any other way right now. It'll be all right, really. I read about something like this in Mama's books." He waved a hand towards the rough-hewn overstuffed book shelves on the far side of the small bedroom, the once proud possessions of their late mother.

"She always loved her stories." His voice took on a softer tone when he spoke of her. "Do you remember when she used to read to us when we were little?"

Jessica nodded. She remembered so many things

about her mother, the raven-haired woman who smelled of lavender and whose sparkling laughter could light up a room. A lump formed in her throat when she remembered how she had died a few weeks after Grace was born. Influenza, the doctor told them.

"She loved them books and one has stories from the Civil War. Did you know there was women who snuck along with soldiers on both sides? They dressed as men and went with their husbands because they didn't want them to go alone or to be left behind. All you have to do is keep your head down and pretend for a few weeks or so. That's how long before the Doc says I'll be back up good as new. You go and hold my place and I'll come along once I'm mended. Then you can come back here to Grammy and the kids."

Her head began to reel the first moment he started laying it all out. It was the most outrageous, most terrifying idea she had ever contemplated, spending weeks masquerading as a man in a camp full of men.

"You'll be Jess Newman so it's not really a lie," Jesse cajoled. "Your given name is Jessica and mine's Jesse. Either one of us could go by Jess and it would be true, wouldn't it? When they ask for Jesse Newman, you just say, 'I'm Jess,' and that's it. You keep your head down low and drop your voice when you do have to speak. You'll need to wear a cap. Here, I'll lend you one of mine. You can wear a wrap around your womanly part up top under your shirt or maybe wear two shirts. Keep your cap pulled down low over your eyes, like this. See?"

He sat up awkwardly in the bed with the heavy cast on his leg and demonstrated his best jaunty look, hat low on his brow. "Don't say much and keep some dirt on your face. I'll cut your hair short before you go and...why you looking at me like that? You can do this, I tell you. I already passed their physical exam and they took my picture but our faces are enough alike, you can pass. Nobody'll probably look that close anyway. You know you could outrun every boy in school except me, and truth be told, there was a couple of days you come close to that. I know you can out swim us all down there on the Eleven Point any day and you can outwork about any man I know, can't you?"

She smiled and ducked her head in spite of her fears. Much as she hated the whole idea, the more he talked the more something about it began to sound alarmingly appealing. What was it Grammy always said: "Be careful what you pray for."

In short order, Jessica Newman had embarked on the greatest adventure of her twenty years.

After two miserable weeks in a training camp in the far southwest part of the state, Jessica was happy to be on a train again. She was truly sick of living in drafty tents, heated with Sibley wood burning stoves. She'd heard some of the others joke that the stoves were left over from the Civil War and no warmer than she felt a great many days, she believed it. Things were a might better after she managed to lay hands on an extra blanket but it was cold comfort compared to Grammy's warm quilts. Still, they had more food, even if it was army rations on their mess table on any given day than she might see in a week at home. More than once, she wished she had a way to wrap some of it up and send it home to Jesse, Grammy, Gabe and Grace.

Loneliness and the fear of discovery had kept her on edge and all but silent those first two weeks. She wondered at times if her heart would survive. It raced so, every time an officer glanced her way or another recruit spoke to her. By the time she left the training site with a new assignment, she was praying constantly just to get through another day.

She wasn't really clear on what might happen if she was discovered. She could well imagine, however, in addition to the shame and embarrassment involved, they would simply boot her out the front gate, leaving her with no money, no food and worst of all, no way to get back to Riverton. Of course, her mind also drifted on to the worst of circumstances and it occurred to her they might even put her in jail. She wasn't sure what they might charge her with but either way, it wasn't as if she could call home and ask someone there to send her money because they didn't have any either! She simply had to make this work until Jesse could come and relieve her.

The soft drawl of the young man seated next to her kept her from drifting off to sleep despite the rocking rhythm of the steel wheels spinning over the rails beneath their feet.

Percy Lee Jackson had chattered almost non-stop as fast as he had taken the seat next to her before the train pulled out of the station at Springfield. He had been at a different training camp. Now, however, the native of southeast Missouri--where did he say? Pemiscot County in the Missouri bootheel? Now, like her and all the rest of the passengers in this car, they were traveling replacements for the Civilian Conservation Corps. They were easily recognized in their old-style green army uniforms, left over from the Great War. The uniforms were rough and blatantly ugly but at least they made it easier for her to blend into the group. With the baggy pants and an extra cotton shirt underneath the uniform shirt, she could keep her true gender under wraps without too much effort.

"So what did you say your name was again?" the voice with the unmistakable twang asked.

"Jess." She gave him the simplest answer she could and hoped he might notice how heavy her eyelids were getting. "Jess Newman."

"Jess Newman? Is that all? My name's Percy Lee, Percival really, after my great-grandfather who was a general in the Confederate army. Just about everybody has two names where I come from, like my little brother, Charles Ray and my mother, Mary Lou and my daddy, Jimmy Don. You don't have but one name?"

"Yes, I have a middle name."

"Well, what is it?"

She yawned as she mumbled, "Jessica Ren—" Her voice caught in her throat. She doubled over and began to cough violently.

"You all right? You choke on something?" Percy Lee's concern was genuine.

"No, I'm fine. I'm fine." She held up a hand in a motion of surrender. She took a deep breath and reminded herself sharply to be more careful and to keep her voice pitched deliberately low. "Percy Lee, I'm going to the room in the back, the bathroom."

Jessica scooted up the aisle between the paired seats and quickly locked herself in the passenger car's single rest room. As she latched the door with a resounding thud, she tried desperately to calm her out-of-control heartbeat. Leaning against the gently rocking wall, she reveled in the security of a few protected moments where she didn't have to worry about being discovered.

The developments of the modern train still fascinated her and she smiled as she read the sign above the commode that admonished all passengers Do Not Flush While Train Is Standing in the Station. She ran water in the tiny wash basin and rinsed her face, drying with the plush paper towel she pulled from the wall dispenser.

Back at her seat, the fatigue won out. Before her seat companion could begin anew, she opened the conversation. "Percy Lee, I'm really tired. If you don't mind, I'm going to catch a few winks before we get to....what's the name of this place we're going again?"

"Bennett Spring. The CCC Camp at Bennett Spring, outside of Lebanon, wherever that is. You go ahead and get some sleep. This train does sorta feel like a rocky-horse, don't it? Except, of course, for all the noise. Maybe I'll try it myself."

That would be so nice, Jessica thought to herself as she closed her eyes in earnest. She was thankful for a few more moments of privacy. Jessica Renee indeed, her thoughts drifted off as she fell asleep. That's just what she needed to tell someone these days. How does a male CCC recruit explain away a name like that?

CHAPTER 3

Jessica awoke with a start as Percy Lee half-whispered, leaning over her, "I think we're here." The train had stopped and others in their passenger car were climbing to their feet. She pulled her rucksack from beneath her seat and slung it over her shoulder as did many of the others. She had two clean uniform shirts, an extra pair of trousers, and a couple of pairs of undershorts and shirts—all government-issued clothing—a comb, a toothbrush and two cinnamon-dusted cookies wrapped in a scrap of brown paper.

Out on the platform, the sign on the end of the station house clearly identified the station as Lebanon, Missouri. Jessica pulled the paper containing the cookies from her bag and handed one to Percy Lee.

"Hey, thanks, Jess. What do you figure comes next?" he asked and took a bite.

As fast as the question was asked, the answer appeared in the long, lean form of Captain Wilbur Smith.

"Recruits, 'tention!"

The uniformed young men scrambled into formation as they had learned in training camp. Despite the two weeks of instruction, it was apparent that military precision and its inherent discipline were still new concepts for this group.

"Bus is to the right." The captain's voice sounded again. "Line up at the door and get aboard!"

Jess and Percy Lee trailed along close to the rear of the group. She shoved the rest of the cookie in her mouth in an effort to make certain she wasn't breaking any sort of military protocol. There was no telling what type of officer this captain might be.

"Come on, girls." His use of the term snapped Jessica's head around until she saw the little smile on his face as his eyes traveled to the knot of recruits already tangled up at the dark green door ahead. "Let's go here." He pushed his way through the group and climbed the steps into the ramshackle army bus. "Inside, inside," he directed, tucked in close by the driver.

As the bus filled, Jessica began to wonder if there would be room for all of them. She and Percy Lee found themselves stuffed together in one of the front seats as the vehicle reached capacity.

The captain picked up a clipboard from a rusty wire basket attached to the dashboard and began reading off names.

"Harrison, Carl; Hollister, Stuart; Jackson, Percival…" Jessica listened as he got closer to hers and to the answers coming from all over the bus.

"Here."

" Here."

" Here."

"Newman, Jesse."

"Here," she answered in her best lowered voice while keeping her eyes on the bus floor.

The captain completed his list and checked off the last name. "Sergeant O'Hara," Capt. Wilbur Smith turned to the driver. "Let's go!"

The old bus engine coughed to life with a low rumble and the vehicle pulled away from the railroad tracks.

Jessica's head whirled as she tried to see everything at once from the bus window. She glimpsed a sign advertising Nelson's Dream Village, another pointing the way to the Lyric Theatre and yet another with an arrow pointing straight ahead— Bennett Spring State Park, 12 miles.

In short order, she found herself swaying and holding on tight as the rickety bus careened around the curves of the hilly gravel road. The sunshine poured in the westbound front windshield but Jess tried to concentrate on the cool air coming through the door that was cracked halfway open. The many shades of green that extended in waves along the road would have provided great comfort and added to the joy of this new adventure on most days, but not today.

Breathe deep. Breathe slow, she told herself after a short while and closed her eyes. She tried to will herself not to be sick.

"Better slow down a little, Sergeant," the captain warned. "We've got a heavy load here—"

"Now, Captain, I've run this road a lot of days and I know it seems pretty rough but it's not all that bad. Our turn off is just around this next curve."

Jessica took another shaky breath, praying that they would indeed be stopping soon. Oh, heavenly days, she did not want to start off in this new place by throwing up in front of her new commanding officer! She noticed that Percy Lee's incessant chatter had ceased. She glanced his way in time to see him double over and at the same time, she heard an oath from the driver as he stomped on the brakes. The bus slid sideways, spinning for a split second before slamming into a solid barrier that had suddenly appeared in the roadway.

An alarmingly familiar shriek was followed by numerous grunts and groans behind her. The driver gave a violent shove on the shiny vertical handle halfway between himself and the steps and the door flew wide open. She tumbled out of the bus behind the captain and Percy Lee, who was suddenly on his knees, depositing his last meal in the roadside grass.

Jessica struggled to see through the bright sunlight reflecting off the cloud of dust that filled the air from the road gravel and the hay that surrounded them on all sides. The nose of the bus was buried in a stack of more hay and a large wagon lay on its side across the road. A teenage boy peeked out from the disheveled stacks of hay with a tentative plea. "Grandpapa?"

Jessica pulled herself to her feet as she located the source of that painful sound she heard as the bus and wagon collided. She scampered across the road to the front of the wagon where a pair of panic-stricken horses struggled in the twisted mess of leather, chains and straps that had once been their harness.

"Easy now, boy. Easy. It's gonna be all right. You hold on there now," she cooed, while running her hands quickly over the pair of black geldings, one of which was standing. The other was on the ground, caught up in the trace chains, with the single tree pressing deeply into his hip. His eyes roamed wild but he followed Jessica's movements as she mustered all her strength to unhook the confining chains quickly. She continued to talk softly, calming the stricken horse which waited until she grasped his halter lightly and then he scrambled unexpectedly to his feet.

A battered black pickup truck stopped behind the bus and a tall man ran towards the chaos.

"Grandpapa?" the boy called again.

"Joey?" The newest arrival hurried to the boy, still in the hay. "Are you all right?"

"I don't see my grandfather. He was driving our

wagon when this happened…"

"Josef!" The tall man let out a loud call and turned back towards the others.

"Who? Who are you looking for?" Captain Smith began to try to take charge once again.

"Josef Schultz, the old man who drives this wagon. This is his grandson, Joey. What happened here?"

"I'm not sure," the captain stammered. "We came around the curve and apparently the wagon was in the road."

"We were crossing is all," the boy spoke up. "We didn't see no one comin'. Where is my grandpapa?"

"Josef!" The driver of the pickup hollered again and a groan could be heard from the far side of the road.

The sergeant ran in the direction of the sound. "He's over here!"

The others followed and gently lifted the old farmer in overalls from the roadside ditch. Another car, this one headed east, stopped on the far side of the heaped hay and a man and his wife came forward.

"Oh, Josef! Joey." The older woman reached out and cupped the boy's face in her palm. "Are you all right, boy?"

"I think so," he answered honestly. "But Grandpapa—"

The old man moaned again as he tried to stand on his own two feet and collapsed back into the arms of his rescuers.

"Josef, you best not strain yourself yet," the first man stated as he helped ease him to a seated position. "Melvin, Harriet. Are you headed to town? Could we send Josef and the boy with you?"

"But of course, Zeb," Harriet answered immediately. "If you can help us get him into the back seat, we'll take them both to the doctor, won't we, Melvin?"

Her husband nodded as the two neighbors cautiously eased the old farmer to his feet and helped him into the waiting vehicle. Several of the bus passengers quickly cleared a path along the edge of the roadway for the car to pass.

"We'll take care of the horses, Joey." Zeb roughly patted the teen's hand that held on tight to the edge of the car door's window as the car pulled away. "I'll get them down to my place."

"Thank you, Mr. Darling," the worried boy called back. "You tell my grandmama?"

"Yes, Joey. I'll see to it."

Jessica had both horses on their feet, still trembling but relatively calm when she heard the captain's voice behind her.

"Captain Wilbur Smith," he introduced himself to the pickup truck driver.

"Zeb Darling," the other man returned with a handshake. "You got yourself quite a mess here. All your boys in good shape?"

"Yes, as far as I can see. A few bumps and bruises

is all, nothing we're not used to. I sure hope that old man will be all right." He looked down the now vacant road as the last of the dust settled from the departing car.

"Old Josef is a pretty tough farmer. As long as nothing inside is broke, I'd say he'll be fine in a few days. What happened here?" He repeated his earlier question.

"Well, I think..." He hesitated and cast an eye in the sergeant's direction.

"We came around the curve like the boy said," the sergeant interjected, "and that dadburn wagon was right in the middle of the road. There was nowhere to go, I tell you."

"It would seem," the captain tried again. "I imagine that was the way of it. I wasn't honestly looking at the road at the time, so I can't say for certain."

"Well, it wouldn't surprise me none." Zeb shook his head. "Old Josef is well known around here for still driving as if he owns the road. A couple of us have tried to warn him to be more careful, but you know how it is sometimes with the old folks...." He left the statement unfinished and grinned at the captain.

"I appreciate that," the captain nodded, happy to avoid any controversy over who was at fault. "Boys, let's get this wagon righted!" the captain called over his shoulder. "And the rest of you, clear that road. Move that hay off to the sides!"

Two dozen green-clad young men scurried at the sound of his orders. A few easily flipped the wagon upright onto its four wheels with a loud clatter which once again made the skittish horses jump sideways but Jessica kept a firm grip on them both. Together, the men rolled the wagon to the far side of the road and up onto a grassy bank. Zeb climbed aboard, set the brake, and jumped back to the ground. Jessica followed slowly behind, leading both horses.

"Now, you seem to have taken those two well in hand, young feller," Zeb commented, looking over at her. "They are a fine pair."

"Oh, yes," Jessica nodded. "They are still shook up and this one, his right knee and fetlock look to be some swollen but I don't feel nothing broken in there and he's managing. If we can get a hot poultice on it in short order, I'd say he'll be fine."

"You know horses then," Zeb stated.

"Yes sir. We had Perchys a lot like these for years. Percherons, with my father's hauling company. Before," she answered softly.

"Before?"

"Before all these hard times."

"Well, let's see if we can get these two down the road a mile or so to my place."

"Captain." Zeb turned back to Captain Smith who was having a sharp discussion with the sergeant. They stood away from the bus and its passengers who were still milling about. "Captain, if you could lend me this one long enough to get these horses down to my place I'd sure appreciate it. I'll load some of this hay in my truck and take it along with the horses but as much as they've been through, I hate to try leading them tied to the truck. If this young feller could go along—" Zeb veered back, "what's your name, boy?"

"Jess, Jess Newman," she answered. She reconfigured the lines to ride one horse and pony the other alongside. She stepped up on the tail end of the wagon, grabbed a handful of mane and easily swung a leg over the bare back of the uninjured horse. She nudged the horse beneath her with her knees and the black beauties walked towards the two men, who were still discussing their next move.

"Yeah, I suppose that would be all right, considering the circumstances." He gave another stern glance in the sergeant's direction. "Sergeant, let's get the rest of these men loaded back on the bus. A few of you there, load some of that hay into this man's truck. Newman, is it? You go with him and get those horses settled where they need to be. Mr. Darling, you know where our camp is so I trust you'll get him back to us later today once you have things squared away."

"Yes, sir. I can do that. Thank you, Captain. I appreciate it," Zeb answered as he turned towards his truck which now, thanks to the recruits, had a clear roadway once again.

The others, once back on the bus, hooted and hollered at her as the bus passed by and Jessica gave them a little wave but kept her attention focused on her two charges.

She cast her eyes towards the late afternoon sky and gave a silent prayer of thanks. To be riding a fine draft horse slowly down a country road in the warm spring sunshine was, no doubt, a true blessing from God. Just a half hour before she had been fighting not to throw up and now she felt like she had received a reprieve straight from heaven. Zeb Darling drove slowly along the road and she let the horses follow at their own pace. Both seemed much more comfortable now to be walking side by side as they usually did. Jessica's thoughts meandered as well. If only Jesse could see me now…

They traveled down a long gradual hill made ever more lovely by the lush green growth all around that deepened the further they progressed into the burgeoning valley. At a small stand of trees, they passed a wooden sign welcoming all to Bennett Spring State Park. She veered to the left, continuing to follow Zeb's truck, as a swift, picturesque blue-green stream came into view. Her first sight of the spring branch, as the folks of Bennett Spring called it, immediately swept her homeward to the Eleven Point River.

Hers was a true river that included the crystal output of over thirty springs, emptying their living waters into the Eleven Point in the last few miles before it reached Riverton. She had grown up learning to swim in the frigid water that could literally steal your breath away on a cool day or bring you back to life in a chilling moment on a hot one. This stream was a mere fraction of that but just as beautiful, serving as the center point to an entire valley that appeared to be designed specifically to highlight its natural splendor. She had been two weeks in what she had come to consider a dry part of the country. To discover this exquisite blue-green torrent so close to her new location was a welcome sight that brought tears to her eyes.

"You doing all right back there?" Zeb Darling's voice broke through her reverie.

"Yes, sir." Jessica pulled her shirt sleeve hurriedly across her face. "We're fine. These boys are doing real good."

"Glad to hear it." He pulled his head back inside the pickup truck window and waved as he continued down the road.

Jessica kept her eyes on the moving water as they strolled along coming even with the edge of the great languid spring itself. The grand blue hole offered its infinite liquid gift in a manner that made life itself seem to stand still for a few hallowed moments as she and her new companions rode past.

The clip clop of the horses included a few splashes as they took no note of the shallow waters, continuing to follow Zeb's truck and its load of sweet hay. Jessica tried to take in as much of the grandeur of the local landscape as possible. Huge hickories, oaks, elms, thin dogwoods and redbuds and impressive walnut trees covered the valley's hillsides in numerous shades of jade, emerald and chartreuse. And as suddenly as it had begun, her dream ride was over. Zeb Darling's truck pulled to a stop in front of a large cabin with a loft and a hitching rail, running the full length of the wooden front porch. A curl of gray smoke poured from the stone chimney.

"Well, here we are," he said, climbing out of the truck. "You can take the horses right into the barn there." He pointed while still talking. "I'm going inside to let Hannah know what's going on. I'll be along in a few minutes."

"That'll be fine," Jessica answered as she slid to the ground. The horses followed her easily by now and she walked them inside. She tied the horses side by side with their lead lines and then removed each one's bridle, which she hung on the hames of each horse. Next, she unbuckled the hames and slid them back, moved the britchen forward and then pulled the fifty pounds of leather off each horse onto the ground. From there, she struggled to lift each one onto harness pegs she found on the barn side wall. Finally, she removed each horse's collar and added it to the respective harness.

Jessica gave each a small bucket of water she dipped from a rain barrel she found outside the front door. Not too much after so much excitement, she thought. Just enough to calm their nerves.

She found a brush on a shelf near the stalls and began to run it over each one in turn. She talked to them as she worked, continuing the calming routine to help them adjust to the unfamiliar surroundings.

"Who is that? Who's there?"

A new voice surprised her and she whirled to see a man in a deputy sheriff's uniform shirt, standing in the barn doorway.

"Excuse me. I'm just in here, currying the horses for Mr. Darling, Zeb Darling. He asked me to bring them in and—"

"Why, you're one of those CCC fellers, ain't you?" The tall deputy stepped out of the blinding afternoon sunlight in the doorway and Jessica could finally see who was doing the talking.

"Yes. Yes, sir. Jess Newman," she stammered and turned back to the horse she was working on.

"Whose horses are these? Well, what the heck!" He stopped and then answered his own question. "Why, this is Josef Schultz's team! What are they doing here?"

"There was an accident up on the road coming from town." Jessica hesitated. She hated to be the one making the explanations and the last thing she wanted was to be talking to the law. Don't say too much, Jesse's advice echoed in her memory.

"Oh, hello, Benji." Zeb Darling came up behind him and it was then that Jessica could see the strong resemblance between the two—the same sandy hair and mustache, same gentle blue eyes that topped an angular handsome face. "I see you found Jess here, working on the horses. Ol' Josef finally pulled in front of somebody today out there on the main road, don't you know. It's been a long time coming, sad to say. Melvin and Harriet Miller came along and took him on to the doctor in town as he was pretty banged up. Joey was with him, too, but he looked like he was doing all right, just worried about his grandpa. Guess the young ones bounce back quicker from the likes of that sort of thing. I pulled up right after it happened and told Joey I'd bring the horses on down here for now and see to them. Looks like Jess is doing a fine job of that already."

Jessica bobbed her head with a smile in silent answer. Ben picked up a curry comb and started in on the other horse.

"So you say Josef is hurt?" he continued the conversation with his father.

"Well, hard to say," Zeb shrugged. "He was thrown from the wagon a good distance so he could be stove up pretty bad at his age. We got him on his feet and into Melvin's car without too much trouble so hopefully he'll be fine in a few days."

"I'm still not clear." Ben stopped for a moment and glanced in Jessica's direction. "How did the CCC get involved?"

"Oh, I didn't tell you? Their bus is the one that come around the bend and smacked into Josef's wagon. This young feller was on the bus and had these horses under control faster than they can run. I asked the CCC captain if'n I couldn't just borry him for a little while longer to get 'em down here and settled."

"Lucky for ol' Josef there was somebody there to care for his horses," Ben commented as he went on brushing. "They've been the prize-winnin' pullin' team at the county fair now for years." He directed his last comment to Jessica.

"Lucky for the horses, you mean." Zeb added with a smile.

Lucky for me, Jessica thought to herself as she ran her hand over the smooth withers of the horse she had been brushing.

"Let's see," Ben continued. "This is Frankie and Johnny. Frankie here has a lump on his forehead from where he was cut as a colt. Ol' Josef says that's the easy way to tell them one from another."

"Frankie and Johnny, huh?" Jessica grinned.

"Here's what you need, Zeb." A woman appeared at the barn door with a steaming pot in one hand and long strips of ragged cloth hanging from her apron pocket.

"Hannah, this here is Jess Newman, with the CCC. He's the one that ordered up a poultice for the one horse's leg there." Zeb directed his wife towards the young recruit.

"Well, then Jess, is it? All I had was some squash left from last fall but it's been in the root cellar so I scooped out the inside and heated it up on the stove. If you wrap it up with these rags, it should do the trick."

"Yes, ma'am," Jessica answered as she dipped her hand into the warm stringy mush. "If you don't mind, I'll use a little of that bran mash I seen in the barrel over there." Jessica added a handful of the brown feed and stirred it all together. When she had it the consistency she wanted, she began to plaster the mixture around the knee and ankle of the horse she now knew as Frankie. She wrapped the injured leg with the rag strips as Hannah handed them to her.

"Dinner's almost ready, boys. You will stay and eat with us, Jess." It was a statement, not a question.

"Well, ma'am, I dunno." Jessica tried to think of a quick excuse. The more time she spent around anyone, especially another woman, the more she feared discovery.

"Here now, you got to eat, young man, and I can't imagine your captain objecting to you getting a home-cooked meal before we drop you off down at the camp below. It might be awhile before you get another one."

The idea of not having to line up for chow at a mess tent as well as the promise of anything home-cooked was overwhelming. "All right." Jessica decided not to argue. "I just don't want to be too late getting to the camp is all."

"Not to worry," Zeb added.

The tantalizing aromas of squirrel stew topped with baking powder dumplings and blackberry cobbler filled the house and drew Jessica in as irresistibly as a hummingbird to spring blossoms.

"Are you really with the CCC? Where do you come from? What do you do down there at the camp?" Blue-eyed freckle-faced Esther was all breathless questions as fast as her father finished the evening blessing over their dinner.

"Esther, slow down," her mother chided. "Let the

boy eat first."

"It's all right, ma'am." Jessica grinned in spite of her own nervousness. She could imagine Gabe or Grace having the same reaction if a stranger had arrived at their table under similar circumstances. Still, she thought as she took in the flavor of the first spoonful of rich stew and delicate dumpling, it had been a long time since such fine fare had graced their table at home.

"I'm from Riverton, a little town on the Eleven Point River the other side of West Plains," she attempted to answer Esther's questions in order. "I've only been with the CCC a couple of weeks so I don't really have any kind of real job with them yet. Guess that's what I'm a-fixing to do here, find out exactly what they want me to do."

"Riverton? And what do you and yours do in Riverton?" Hannah asked casually.

Jessica glanced at the deputy in uniform once again, sitting next to the woman asking the questions. She worried about answering too many specific questions in front of him and yet she didn't want to be seen as rude by such kind people. It was as if he couldn't stop watching her or was that simply her imagination again? She couldn't tell. What if he decided to make some calls and check her out?

"Oh, these days not much," she continued with a shrug. "My papa had a hauling company there with horses but he died last year working up on the St. Louis waterfront on a tug boat, so now the horses and the company are gone and so is he."

"I'm so sorry," was Hannah's instant response. "It was plain to see you knew your way around the horses out there. I certainly hope Josef's horses will be well enough and him too. Something to add to my prayer list, that's for certain."

"You keep a prayer list, ma'am?" Jessica looked up from her steaming dinner bowl. "My grammy does, too. She says she tries to make it a blessing list as much as possible, but sometimes these days that's not so easy."

Hannah laughed. "I'd say that's true enough, Jess. Do you write to your grandmother or does she write to you?"

Jessica dropped her eyes and quickly swallowed the last bite of the delicious stew. "Not so much. My brother, he's the letter writer of the family. I'm hoping to write home soon and tell her I'm here and then maybe they can write to me and tell me the news from home."

"Ma, I hate to rush you," Ben spoke up, "but I'm going to have to move along if I'm going to meet that Dallas County deputy down at the county line and pick up that prisoner they're transferring to us. That's the only reason I got to come out and have supper with you all tonight and I really want a big piece of that blackberry cobbler before I go."

Hannah grinned at her son's impatience. "I understand, Benji," she answered as she stood up, turning back from the stove. "Jess, are you interested in blackberry—"

She was interrupted by a heavy knock on the front

door. "Who could that be?"

Zeb got up from the table quickly and opened the door and then stumbled backwards in surprise. "What in the name of glory—"

A rough-bearded man with long hair and tattered worn clothes took a tentative step inside. "I didn't want to come like this…" His voice was low but his eyes instantly riveted on Hannah who was still standing at the stove, digging out spoonfuls of blackberry cobbler.

"Oh my heavens. Look at you!" Hannah dropped her spoon and scooted across the kitchen to embrace the new arrival. "Look at you! Aren't you a sight?"

"Yes, ma'am, I expect I am." A small smile escaped him. "I've been on the road quite a few days now, hitching back here from western Oklahoma. Tain't a lot of people want to give you a ride if'n they don't know you. And I don't imagine I look like much more than road trash these days anyway."

"Well, never mind that. We got dinner on the table so you just get yourself in here and get you some and we'll worry about all the rest later on. Do you have a bag or anything with you?" She looked behind him as if she expected such things to simply materialize as she spoke of them.

"No, ma'am. Just a bedroll I'll leave out here on the porch, if you don't mind, 'cause it ain't none too clean."

"Fine, fine. Come on in and wash your hands and I'll fill you a plate."

The deputy got to his feet and moved over to the stranger to offer a handshake and clapped his other hand onto the man's shoulder, raising a tiny cloud of dust as he did so. "We've been wondering about you for awhile now out there in that dust bin called Oklahoma." Ben grinned as he welcomed him.

"That it is," he sighed as he slipped off his cap, ran a hand through his long blond hair and hung the cap up on the pegs by the door.

"Sir." The new arrival bobbed his head in Zeb's direction, who seemed dumbstruck at the sight of him. Jessica remembered at the last minute, to stand as a man and offer a handshake to the newcomer, who sat down beside her.

Hannah returned to dishing out saucers of cobbler and another bowl of squirrel stew and dumplings while making introductions. "This is Jess Newman, one of the CCC boys working down in the valley. Jess, this is our oldest son, Jake."

CHAPTER 4

Upon arrival at the CCC camp proper, Jessica discovered the others had already been delegated to various work details to begin the next day. They had also been assigned bunks in one of the CCC barracks. A grinning Percy Lee pulled his rucksack off the lower bunk opposite the one he was sitting on as she made her way into the barracks where she had been directed.

"I saved you a bunk, friend."

"Thanks." She ducked her head shyly and collapsed onto the bed in the corner.

"Hey, you're welcome," he replied. "I had an upper bunk at the last camp and that's not so hot, let me tell you."

"Oh yeah? How come?" Her last post had been a cot in a tent.

"'Cause when you get back to your bunk at the end of the day and you're so tired you can barely make it in the door, climbing up into that bunk is just about more than you can stand!" He laughed out loud at his own joke.

The next morning Jessica found herself assigned to a crew that stayed busy all day, running a pair of cement mixers and hauling the freshly mixed mortar one wheelbarrow at a time over to those who were laying stones into place at the base of the new tourist cabins. She was familiar with hand crank mixers, like the ones she had seen on occasion in Riverton, but these were different. They were the first gasoline-powered ones she had ever encountered and she was soon thankful for the intensive labor-saving motors. Still, the shoveling of sand, lime and cement and the hauling of the heavy wet mixture quickly took its toll. Jesse's words echoed in her tired brain....'You can outwork about any man I know.'

She wondered how much longer she would last at this rate. More importantly, would she last until Jesse could get here? Each wheelbarrow full of mortar felt heavier than the last, she thought as she began to push another towards the waiting stone masons.

"Hey, kid," a familiar voice called from behind her. "What was your name...Newman, that's it. Jess Newman. Hold up there."

Jessica set the wheelbarrow down carefully and turned, keeping her eyes on the ground. Once again, a face-to-face encounter and the fear of discovery was nearly overwhelming. "Yes, sir," she answered demurely as Captain Wilbur Smith approached.

"Look, Newman, you were the last one in the other night so I put you down as a floater."

"Sir?" With an effort, she pulled her eyes up to his face, searching for answers.

"A floater." A half smile crossed his face while he flipped through a half dozen sheets of paper pinned to the clipboard in his hand. "It means you'll float from one detail to another as we need an extra hand. You know how it is, last one in gets the leftovers," he added in his best apologetic fashion. "Look at it this way, you won't have time to get bored and besides, from what I saw with you and those horses, you seem to be able to adapt pretty quickly to the situation."

She shrugged with a smile. "I suppose. Sir?"

"Yes?"

"Have you heard any more about the old farmer on the hay wagon?"

"No." He frowned at his paperwork as he made a couple of notes. "But that's a good question. I'll check on him and find out and I'll try to let you know. Would be good local relations, anyway," he muttered, more to himself than to the recruit before him.

"I'd appreciate it." She picked up the wheelbarrow again, eager to be on her way and pleased to know she wouldn't be hauling mortar for the whole of the next few weeks.

It was late Thursday afternoon and Deputy Ben Darling was headed towards his parents' home above Bennett Spring once again. He wasn't alone today, however and he hoped his friend's presence wouldn't be a problem. He knew his mother wouldn't care that he was bringing along another mouth to feed and he doubted that his father would either, but Becky might have a different opinion.

"I really appreciate you taking me along to dinner," Cletus Meyers, one of his fellow sheriff's department employees, broke into Ben's distracted thoughts. "I don't get a lot of dinner invitations." He grinned from the passenger seat of Ben's car.

"Who does?" Ben nodded in agreement. "Besides, you said you needed to come out and check on your uncle's stock while he's in Kansas City, right? I figure we might as well ride out here together."

"Sounds good to me," Cletus agreed readily. "So we going to eat first? I mean, I can go over after we eat. Depending on how much Uncle Jack got done before he left, I might just have you drop me off and I'll spend the night there and catch up to you tomorrow. What do you think?"

Ben shrugged as they headed down the hill towards the park entrance and the spring. "I think we'll go by home first and then I can drive you over later or just let you take the car. It don't really matter to me."

Cletus sat up straight and stuck his head out the window to catch the fresh breeze in his face. "Whatever you decide. You're driving."

They climbed out of the car and stepped up onto the front porch of the Darling house. "Hey, Ma," Ben called out as he opened the door. "I brought company."

"Well, hello, Cletus." Hannah Darling looked up from the catfish she was frying in a heavy iron skillet on the wood stove. "Haven't seen you since....hmm, when was it? Late this winter when Benji started at the sheriff's department and I stopped by?"

"Yes, ma'am." Cletus pulled off his hat as he entered the home and nervously rolled the brim in his hands.

"Mr. Darling, good to see you." Cletus nodded to Zeb, sitting behind his newspaper. "Becky, it's nice to see you, too." His tone sweetened ever so slightly, but it was enough that she noticed as she looked up from the cast iron skillet of fresh baked cornbread she was pulling from the hot oven.

"Well, Cletus, what a surprise." Becky glanced over her shoulder and then shot her brother a squinted glare of aggravation. "How've you been?"

"Oh, I'm okay." He rolled the hat brim even faster. "How about you?"

"Fine." She stood up straight, after closing the oven door. "Fine and ready." She turned towards him, lacing her fingers across her enlarged middle.

"Yes, I see." He grinned in slight embarrassment. "I'd heard you and J.C. were a-waiting these days. Congratulations."

"Thank you, Cletus."

"So you've been with the sheriff's department a long time now, haven't you?" Hannah turned the fish, pulling out the finished golden pieces to drain on a large platter lined with strips of newspaper.

"Yes, ma'am, over ten years now. Ever since that first summer Becky went to work at the Brice Inn. I worked as a road deputy for a lot of years but these days I mostly work close in to town, tending the jail and serving papers and such," he shrugged.

"Can I take this?" Eleven year old Esther tugged at his hat. "I can hang it up for you."

He reluctantly released the hat and she hung it on the pegs beside the door.

"Come on." Ben pushed him towards the back bench of the table. "We'll have a seat back here and stay out of the way."

"You can wash up first." His mother re-directed them past the kitchen sink. "We'll eat before long."

They made it through dinner without difficulty but Cletus was anxious to check out his uncle's farm situation. Ben tossed him the car keys. "You can take the car and go on over. Or do you need help?"

"No, I don't need no help. I appreciate you giving me a ride out here, but what about later tonight or tomorrow?"

"Well, I ain't going anywhere else tonight, Cletus. You can just bring the car back tomorrow morning."

"So how's ol' Jack Kingman doing?" Zeb Darling spoke up. "Even though he lives down the lane at the top of the hill on the road past the church, I don't see him much."

"He's good," Cletus nodded. "He mostly stays back on the farm, raising a few head of cattle. I promised to check on them for him while he's up visiting and going to his son's wedding in Kansas City."

"Your cousin getting married? Which one?" Hannah asked as she cleared the dishes.

"Jackie, ma'am, Jack Junior. He's the oldest, a good fifteen years older than me but getting married for the first time ever. He's been up there in Kansas City now for years, working in the stockyards."

"Well, I guess that's good, if he likes it," she added, trading a brief glance with her son.

And with that, Cletus accepted Ben's offer, excused himself, thanked the Darlings for dinner and headed across the valley.

"I can't believe you brought him along." Becky shook her head as fast as she heard Ben's car start up outside. "What were you thinking, Benji?"

"I knew you'd have to say something." He swung around to face her in his own defense. "I was thinking that he works hard and he don't get out much and he's been awful darn nice to me at the new job."

"You know what I mean!" she hissed back.

"Yeah, I know what you mean. It ain't my fault or

maybe his neither that he still carries a torch for you, even if you have been married nearly ten years now. He ain't never married and maybe he never will or—." He shrugged. "Maybe he'll be like his cousin and get married in another fifteen years. Who knows? But in the meantime, it don't mean I can't be friends with him. I ain't bringing him out here often and anyway, like he said, he had to come check on his uncle's cattle."

"Oh, children, stop arguing," Hannah intervened as she put together the batch of cream to be churned into butter, which she turned over to Esther. Becky had already begun to work on her baby quilt squares and tonight her mother joined her in the effort. "Cletus is always welcome here. He's been kind to Benji. He was kind to Jake years ago when he…" She stopped speaking with an exhausted sigh. "Well, he's always been kind to this family and he's always welcome at our table and that's that."

Jessica slipped along through the woods behind the Civilian Conservation Corps barracks. After three days at Bennett Spring, she was starting to feel like she might actually live through this experience. She certainly appreciated sleeping in a real building. The barracks the CCC had built upon their arrival at Bennett Spring two years ago were so much better than the damp tents at her last assigned location. She had also discovered plenty of food was available to the CCC workers here. Tonight, however, she had her mind on yet another necessity.

Cleanliness next to Godliness, Grammy often said.

Jessica hadn't forgotten about God and so far, despite her occasional panic, she was certain He hadn't forgotten about her. Now about that cleanliness...

A nice warm day was coming to an end and the evening air was still heavy with the early summer humidity. Tonight was to be a near full moon. She reached the new concrete bridge and slipped across, dodging the scraps of construction material that still lay scattered about the area. The bridge was not yet open to vehicle traffic but more than finished enough for a single girl to slip across in the twilight. She was so busy anticipating, she almost didn't notice the vehicle speeding along the dirt road towards her until it was too late. The large dark car was moving fast, especially for one running without lights despite the quickly fading daylight, a fact the driver realized too late. Its speed was of no help, however, when it clipped an unseen hole at the edge of the road and spun out of control. Jessica quickly dove towards the dam side of the bridge, crouching out of sight past the end of the bridge. The car struck the east end of the bridge head on and came to an abrupt stop.

Jessica peeked around the end of the bridge as two men tumbled from the steaming car, cursing one another and their situation.

"If you can't drive no better than that—" the one began accusing the other.

"Me? You was the one said don't put on the lights or else...dang it, Herbie! Somebody's coming!" They both whirled and the driver dove back into the passenger side, pulled out a heavy canvas bag and hurriedly stuffed it into the arms of the other.

"Quick, Herbie! Take this and get around the end of the bridge! Don't make a sound! I'll take care of this."

The man with the bag quickly ducked out of sight, directly opposite of Jessica, as the lights of the approaching car lit the scene. Jessica saw the new car pass by and then stop in the center of the not-yet-completed concrete bridge. As the driver stepped out, she saw the large gold star on the side of his car door. It looked like the car Deputy Ben Darling was driving a few evenings ago when he gave her a ride to her new barracks but he certainly wasn't the driver tonight.

"Good evening." The driver of the damaged car spoke up as the newcomer approached.

"What's going on here? Having some trouble, I see."

"Yes, I guess we, uh, my tire caught the edge of a hole on the side of the road, I'm afraid, and—"

"And smacked into the brand new bridge! Why, they don't even have it done yet and now you've gone and hit it." Cletus Meyers shook his head. "Well, I guess you're all right but now your car here, on the other hand…" Cletus knelt down to have a closer look at the front fender.

"You got a tire iron handy?" He asked the first driver as he stood up.

"Why, uh, I'm sure I do…somewhere." The other

man began to shovel furiously through the scattered contents of the trunk of his car. "Here, I think this is what you mean."

Cletus took the heavy iron instrument and headed back towards the front of the vehicle where he proceeded to pry the bent fender away from the right front tire.

Jessica watched momentarily as Cletus worked on the vehicle but behind her, echoing through the first of the bridge's three arches, she could hear strange scraping sounds coming from the far side of the bridge. What was that other man, Herbie, doing over there, she wondered.

"There you go. Try backing it up and see if that won't work a little better now," Cletus said as he returned the tire iron to the driver.

The man tossed it into the front seat and quickly climbed in beside it. The car started immediately and he slowly backed it up as Cletus came up beside him.

"Uh, thank you. Thank you so much." The driver laughed as he shook the deputy's hand, reaching through the driver's window.

"No problem," he told him. "Deputy Cletus Meyers, happy to be of service. You okay now?"

"Oh, I'm fine, officer," the man stammered, still smiling. "Just a little shook up is all. Think I'll just sit here a moment or two and get my bearings, if you don't mind."

"Not a problem," Cletus told him. "Here. This

bridge ain't even in use yet. Watch and you'll see me cross up yonder, just below the new dam on the flange bridge. That's where you need to go. This one will be open soon but not yet."

"Well, thank you, Deputy. I appreciate the help."

"I'll be on my way then."

Deputy Cletus Meyers backed up and wheeled around towards the old bridge to negotiate the crossing. Jessica scrambled around to the backside of her hiding place to make certain the deputy's headlights didn't catch her, crouched behind the end of the bridge. Once the deputy's car disappeared around the bend, the other man reappeared from his side of the bridge. The full moon Jessica had been expecting was already up, bathing the entire area in its pale blue light. As the man climbed back into the passenger seat, Jessica thought he looked like he was streaked with dirt but she gave it little thought. The two drove on, this time with their lights on but Jessica lingered in her hiding place at the end of the bridge.

After a few extra minutes and seeing no more activity on the road, the gentle call of the spring branch waters drew her back to her original mission. She crept on, looking for the place she had seen earlier in the day, where the brush grew close down along the water's edge. The place she sought was a short distance above the water fall created by the dam.

The water was cold and brisk but deliciously so. She stripped to the waist in the solitude of the beautiful night beside the moving water. The spring branch babbled along and she was thankful for the opportunity to bathe for the first time in more than a week. She didn't dare risk going to the wash house the men used at their leisure, for fear of being discovered. She and her brother had worked out strategies for coping with many aspects of her secret role but she had not seriously contemplated the difficulty of getting a bath on a regular basis. Here, at least, there was plenty of water, plenty of access as long as she came like this, after dark. She let out a sigh of relief as her mind drifted briefly over the last couple of weeks. How long had it been now? she wondered and, more to the point, how much longer would it be?

The two of them had made all their preparations in secret those last three days before she left. At first, Jesse told her he did not want to tell Grammy anything about where she was going, only that she had run away.

"You know how she is," Jesse warned her. "As like as not, she'll come after you or send the sheriff, telling him to go fetch her granddaughter out of a men's camp!"

"I know, I know," Jessica countered, "but I can't have her thinking I ran off and abandoned her and you and most of all, those two little ones. If that's what you're going to tell her, then I won't go at all and you can't make me!"

After an hour of debate, her brother finally agreed to a letter that she wrote, saying simply she'd found a chance to make some money for the family and she would come home as soon as she could.

"There," she said with more than a note of triumph in her voice as she handed the paper to Jesse, which he faithfully promised to deliver once she was gone. "Now, they don't know nothing but they know too, that I didn't just walk out on them. I could never do that!"

"No," he grinned. "You couldn't. Me neither. This is a better way and besides, it ain't a lie either. You will be sending money home after a little while."

She would have to write soon and let Jesse know where she was now; most importantly, so he would know where to come and find her. As near as she could figure, he would have to take the train from West Plains to Springfield and then Springfield to Lebanon and then...oh, it was too much to think about right now.

Jessica leaned forward and washed her face in the cold clear spring water before dunking her head in. The cold on her scalp made her shiver but that didn't matter. To wash her hair and literally feel clean all over would be so refreshing. She would get warm in short order once she was back in her bunk. She rinsed her hair and stood up to dry off one last time. It still felt so odd, to have such short hair for the first time in her life. Jesse had cut it short that last night before she slipped out in the dark, walking, hitching a ride to West Plains, to use his government-issued train ticket early the next morning.

She heard a rustling behind her in the bushes.

Surely, just some woodland creature, a fox, a raccoon, or even a skunk or deer, she thought as she wrapped her head in her towel and turned towards the underbrush behind her.

Ben was surprised by the approach of car lights as even before Cletus knocked on the door, he recognized the slightly rough-running sound of his own car.

"Didn't expect to see you again 'til tomorrow," Ben said as he opened the door to his friend.

"Well, don't I just feel stupid," Cletus replied with a grin. He took one step past Ben into the house and retrieved his hat still hanging on the peg where it had been placed a couple of hours earlier.

"Esther noticed after you were gone that it was still here but I didn't figure you'd come back for it tonight."

"No, I wouldn't have except I got all the way down to my uncle's gate and remembered that the key he gave me was right here." Cletus bent the inside hat band down and pulled out a small padlock key. "I could have left the car at the gate and walked in but it's another quarter mile and I didn't like the idea of leaving your car out there like that, so far from the house."

"Well, I appreciate that, Cletus. So now what?"

"If'n you don't care, Ben, why don't you just drive me back over there and drop me off? Then you can have your car and come get me tomorrow whenever you're ready to head back to town. I'd sure feel better about it that way, if you don't mind."

Ben shook his head with a smile. "Not a problem, Cletus. Come on. I'll be back shortly, Ma," he called over his shoulder as he pulled the door closed behind them.

He drove Cletus back across the valley and up the hill toward his uncle's farm. Ben glimpsed his friend's face in the moonlight, with his eyes closed and his head leaned back against the car seat.

"Cletus, you all right?" Ben asked.

"Oh, yeah." Cletus made an attempt to sit up straight. "Just tired is all. Got pretty aggravated with myself when I got all the way up to the gate and found out I didn't have the key. Dumb as all get out, don't you know."

"It's okay, not to worry," Ben told him. "At least, it ain't like you left it in town or anything."

"Yeah, that's why I put it in my hat band," Cletus continued, "'cause then I figured I couldn't forget it. There's always a way to forget something, if'n you try hard enough, I guess."

Ben didn't say anything more. After dropping Cletus off at his uncle's farm, he drove back through what had once been the town of Brice. All of the buildings were already vacated, standing abandoned except for the store, the church, the hotel and the mill. He knew it was all slated for demolition by the CCC at some point. He had grown up here and the impending loss of their town had been one of the most difficult parts of the establishment of the park for some of the locals. His sister, Becky, was one of them. Now that the park was officially established, it would all be gone soon. The Bennett family had secured an agreement with the state that bequeathed one acre to the church for as long as it continued to meet. As his father kept making note, everything was changing. The question remained whether those changes would prove to be for the good or the bad.

He pulled his car to the side of the road, near a place where the brush grew down close to the water. This was his favorite spot, just above the dam where he would often catch a glimpse of a beaver or muskrat along the opposite bank. The coming of more people, tourists and even campers as they called the ones who came to pitch a tent or pulling a little trailer behind their vehicle, was likely to make it harder than ever to get a look at Bennett Spring's diminishing wildlife. Even if he didn't see anything tonight, it didn't matter.

The truth was Ben Darling simply wanted a few minutes to sit beside the water and enjoy the clear, quiet night. He had been promising himself the last couple of times he had come back home to dinner that he would do that, take a few minutes and....

Ben heard delicate splashing along the spring branch before he reached the water's edge. He ducked down in the brush and eased forward without making a sound. Could there be a rare deer, drawn to the crystal waters on such a moon-drenched night? Now that would be a treat. Another soundless step or two, and he could see…

Ben Darling stumbled in his haste to back away from the totally unexpected. He had not been seen and startled as he was, he desperately wanted to keep it that way. That certainly wasn't the sort of wildlife he had expected to encounter along the water's edge.

What was she doing out here? Where did she come from? Why was she out here like that? His head was spinning with questions but one thing was certain, the creature who stood up in the pale moonlight, head wrapped in a towel, facing him, was a woman, full grown.

CHAPTER 5

The next morning Jessica awoke feeling so much better. She would have to find a way to bathe in that stream more often, chilly as it was. She stretched before she rolled out of her warm bunk. Waking up clean and warm felt so good and added to her growing sense of confidence, despite the ache in her shoulders that reminded her of all the hard work already behind her. Undoubtedly, there was more to come.

She and Percy Lee made their way to breakfast mess together as was becoming their habit. They each got a metal tray, a knife and fork and waited patiently for whatever the morning fare might be. Today, things seemed to be moving more slowly than ever. When they finally arrived at the serving window, breakfast turned out to be toast smothered in sausage gravy. Some of the others snickered as they spoke in whispers of S.O.S. Slop on a Shingle, Percy told her, also in a hushed voice. Jessica didn't pretend to understand their amusement but she wasn't complaining either. It was hot and steamy and had meat in it. It wasn't Grammy's cooking but with a little salt and pepper, it was more than edible.

Outside, in the early morning sunshine, Jessica headed towards the already chugging mortar mixing machines. She was soon trundling along, wheeling along with her first wheelbarrow full of heavy wet mortar for the day.

"Hey, Newman, Jess Newman."

She turned at the sound of Captain Smith's voice.

"Sir?" She stopped and set down her load.

"Remember I told you I was going to use you as floater?"

"Yes, sir."

"Well, get ready." He flipped through the paperwork on his clipboard. "We were short two men in the mess hall this morning, both in the infirmary. I'm going to need you to go help cook. Can you manage that? Cooking, I mean."

She did her best to hide her smile. "Yes, yes, sir," she answered. "I can help cook. Ain't never cooked for so many, of course, but as long as somebody else can show me...."

"That's the spirit. Okay, I need to run this form up to the boys in A company. Drop your last load of mortar and then meet me up there and I'll get a transfer form filled out for you." He walked away and suddenly turned back.

"Hey, Jess. Something different today?"

"Sir?" Had he noticed something she'd missed? She worried.

"You smell some better today, heh?"

She grinned in spite of her discomfiture. "Finally got a bath...uh, a shower after that long train ride," she muttered.

"Well, glad to hear it. Welcome to the Bennett Spring CCC Camp, kid."

"Yes, sir." She ducked her head and pushed the last load of mortar toward its destination.

Captain Smith grinned to himself as he watched the new recruit walk away. These country kids, so many of them away from home for the first time, didn't even know when to get a shower without their mamas along to tell them. He shook his head as he re-focused his attention on the forms in his hand.

A half hour later, Jessica was walking towards the captain where she saw him standing on the high road, when the deputy's car pulled to a stop not far from the church.

"Good morning, Deputy," Captain Wilbur Smith called out as Ben Darling crossed the gravel road in a few long-legged strides. "And what's the Laclede County Sheriff's Department doing out here this fine morning?"

"Oh, not much. Came out to visit the folks and get some of my ma's home cooking last night. I dropped her off just now over at the hotel to deliver their butter and milk."

"I'd say that would be worth the drive from town," the captain nodded.

"Definitely," Ben agreed. "I eat at the jail or one of the drug store lunch counters most days in town. It's good to get back and get a home-cooked meal, whenever I can."

"Something home-cooked does sound good. Not like there's much chance of me coming across any of that soon," Captain Smith added.

"I suppose that is a problem in your line of work. So how's it all going? My pa says you're making lots of progress in your building projects."

"Oh, we're moving right along. We'd do better if the weather would be more accommodating. I cannot believe how much it rains in this part of the country. I tell you what, I'm thankful our boys are sleeping in barracks and not tents like when they first arrived here."

"Oh, don't judge us too harshly, Captain," Ben grinned. "It has been an unusually wet spring, there is no doubt. All the old-timers have been complaining about it. Makes it awful hard to get crops in the ground, that's for sure."

"Excuse me just a minute, Deputy." The captain turned his attention to the bus-driving Sergeant O'Hara who had approached from the other side, with a handful of papers the captain began to review and sign.

Ben's gaze drifted past the two but riveted on the approaching recruit with the worn gray cap. He was not likely to forget the sight of her in the pale moonlight. His mind had been working overtime, trying to sort it all out ever since last night. He had slept little, despite the comfort of his own bed under the eaves of his parent's home. What was she doing here, and an even more pressing question, what should he do about it? The CCC didn't hire women to work in the field. But then the recruit before him with cement dusted across her cheeks and the bridge of her nose was not dressed as a woman. He caught the glare she shot his way as his eyes met hers, certainly not for the first time.

She returned his stare but inside, the panic returned, causing her heart to race. It was not like he hadn't seen her before, sitting across his mama's table at dinner just a few nights ago. She trembled slightly as she tried to tell herself not to be so mistrusting.

"Good morning, Jess, was it?" He spoke first.

"'Morning, Deputy." She returned with her eyes on the ground. Now what? Her thoughts tumbled, kaleidoscope fashion, one over the other. What did men talk about in a situation like this? She kicked the dirt at her feet but her head snapped up when she heard Sergeant O'Hara call out.

"Jackson, Percy Jackson!" A lone CCC worker, walking at the far side of a large cedar tree in the field between the mill and the church, whirled at the sound of the voice and trotted towards the sergeant.

"Yes, sir." A breathless but ever eager Percy Lee

arrived at the sergeant's side.

"Here. Take these over to the head cook at the mess hall and then this here paperwork goes to..." The sergeant hesitated. "Hold on a second." He turned back to the captain who had resumed his conversation with the deputy.

"Hey, Jess," Percy Lee grinned. "Deputy." He bobbed his head in greeting.

"'Morning," Ben answered, as the captain and the sergeant went back to conferring over their paperwork.

"Percy Lee Jackson." He stuck out his hand in greeting.

"You another one of the new arrivals?"

"Yes, sir. Came in on the train a couple days ago, along with Jess here and a couple dozen others."

"Uh-huh." Ben glanced his way briefly. "I see." He scrambled to think of another general question. Anything to keep them talking, especially her.

"So where do you come from?" He tried to sound like any other friendly local.

"Pemiscot County, down in the bootheel," Percy Lee volunteered in his telltale southern drawl. "I got to say I've picked a lot of cotton over the years but this is my first time building anything. Pretty interesting though." He slid his thumbs into blue jean belt loops that held no belt and rocked back on his heels.

"And you?" Ben echoed again as he looked over at

Jessica.

"Riverton. On the Eleven Point River." She tried to concentrate on Jesse's words of advice. Don't say much and keep some dirt on your face and most people... Well, she had the dirt on her face and she was trying to say as little as possible but this deputy was not making that easy.

"Oh, yeah. Riverton. I remember you saying that at dinner the other night."

"Dinner?" Percy Lee's eyebrows shot up.

"His folks' place is where I took the horses after the wreck with the hay wagon," she offered in explanation.

"Oh, I see. And how them horses doing by now?"

"Better, much better. Joey came around to collect them yesterday. He said his grandpa is back home now, feeling much better although he has a broken arm and a couple of cracked ribs."

"Well, that's good that he ain't any worse than that. So where you from, Deputy?" Percy Lee asked.

"Oh, right here." Ben stamped the ground beneath his feet. "The town of Brice. This was main street," he indicated the roadway before them. "Ain't much left now, except the general store. There's a new store written into the park plans as I understand it so they'll be closing this one soon and moving to the new one once you fellers get it built over yonder." He hitched his thumb towards the fish hatchery.

Jessica's eyes widened despite her personal resolve

to stay uninvolved. "Your town was here where this park is now?"

"Yes, that's the gist of it," he shrugged. "It was never a very big place, just a wide spot in the road really. I used to go to Boy Scout meetings right over there." He grinned at her obvious surprise. "The folks that owned the land, the Bennett family, sold it to the state for Missouri's first state park back ten years or so ago. Little by little, they keep re-shaping it into more of a park all the time. Now in the last couple of years and of course, with you CCC boys here..." He stumbled over the words and glanced sideways at Jessica but she was still captivated by the fact that she was standing on the site of a town that was no more.

"Still, that is so sad!" Jessica exclaimed. "You get a park but you lose your town."

"Now you sound like my father," Ben smirked. "He even tried to organize some of the locals to fight it when the first state folks arrived here to look it all over."

"And what happened?" she asked.

"Pa was mostly worried that he would lose his job as the mailman, I think. They're going to move the Brice Post Office right across the way when they move the store. They'll be operating out of the brand new store building and he's still carrying the mail and—" He hesitated before adding with a sheepish grin, "my sister married one of those state fellers."

"Oh my!" Jessica dropped her eyes back to her

boots and blushed for no discernible reason.

"There you are," Hannah exclaimed as she joined them. "Miz Laraine was happy to get the butter today. She said they've already seen more folks and served more meals this spring than the last couple of years at this time of the year, despite all the rain. That is certainly a good sign, don't you think?"

"I guess so," Ben replied.

"It sounds like maybe more folks are beginning to come to Bennett Spring to visit and if people have money to go traveling, that could be a good thing for all of us."

"Maybe you're right, Ma," he nodded thoughtfully.

"Good morning, Jess. Good to see you again."

"Yes, ma'am. And you." Jessica tipped her cap politely. "This here is Percy Lee."

"Percy Lee," Hannah nodded in his direction. "Nice to meet you."

"So how are you boys doing, working here in the valley? You been away from home long?" Hannah turned to Percy Lee, asking her questions. She made Ben think of Esther at dinner the other night. He put his hand up to his forehead as he realized too late what was coming.

"Been gone from the farm a couple months now, ma'am," Percy Lee answered. "First time I've been very far from the bootheel of southeast Missouri and I got to admit I miss home something fierce some days, but everyone has been real kind so far, so I got no complaints."

"And you, Jess? How are you settling in? Did Benji tell you that Joey came by the house and took his horses home? He says his grandpa is doing much better," she added with a note of motherly concern.

"Yes, ma'am." Jessica again kept her answer and her voice low. She was beginning to wish the captain would finish quickly so she could walk away from this deputy and his mother. They were the nicest people in the world, there was no doubt, but somehow that made the charade she was involved in seem even more awkward, like trying to walk in shoes that were way too small and definitely not her own.

"Well, I tell you what. Benji," Hannah stopped and corrected herself. "Ben here, he comes out to the house each Thursday for supper, so why don't you two come along next Thursday and have dinner with us? Nothing fancy but it'll be home-cooked, that's a promise."

"That's right kind of you, ma'am. What you got to say, Jess? We'll be there, won't we?" Percy Lee answered for both of them while looking at his companion.

Before she could answer, a beat up once red pickup truck swept down from the hill and blew its horn as it pulled to a sudden stop.

"Hey, you all!" The man Jessica had seen as he arrived from Oklahoma at the Darling home a few evenings ago tumbled from the back of the truck while the two men seated in the cab remained inside. He looked different, both better and worse, Jessica thought. His clothes were less dirty and worn but there was still a raggedy appearance about him, not unlike others she had seen who had lost their way in these most challenging times.

"Jake, how are you doing?" Hannah asked, with half a frown on her face as he kissed his mother on the cheek.

"I'm fine, Ma," he answered. "Honest," he added as he noticed her expression.

"I hope so." The doubt was clear to see on her face. "What are you doing? Maybe that's a better question."

"Nothing, really. Me and a couple of the boys are running to town is all. Do you need anything?"

"No, Jake," she snorted as she looked down and shook her head. "We don't need anything."

"Deputy Ben." Jake gave his brother a mock salute. "Are you making your rounds?"

"No, Jake, just visiting. Got to go collect Cletus here in a bit and head back to town."

"Cletus Meyers? Does he still work for the sheriff's department?"

"Yes, he does."

"Wow, I remember him from a-way back. Brings back some not-so-hot memories, heh? Well, the boys are a-waiting. Better git." And with that he turned and hot-footed it back to the waiting truck.

"Ma, I'm sorry." Ben turned towards his mother and

took her gently by the arm.

"Never mind, Benji." She set her jaw and shook off his protection. "Things are what they are and sometimes there's no changing them."

Jessica watched closely, but said nothing.

Percy Lee attempted to breach the awkward moment. "We'd be happy to come to dinner at your house, Mrs. Darling. Won't we, Jess?"

"Well, I don't know…" Jessica tried in desperation to think of a way out.

"Don't know what?" Captain Smith took a step sideways and put himself back into the conversation, as he snapped the paperwork in his hand. He handed papers to Jessica and also to Percy Lee as he spoke. "This your mama, Ben? And she's inviting folks to supper? If you got an invitation like that, Jess Newman, you'd best appreciate it and not be wasting the opportunity."

"Yes, sir." Jessica's confusion deepened. Was there no way to escape?

"We'll be there next week, ma'am. I promise you. Good to meet you, Deputy, and thank you!" Percy Lee giggled with delight and slapped Jessica on the shoulder as they walked away.

Jessica gave a little wave in lieu of saying anything more and looked back over her shoulder as she scurried after Percy Lee.

"He's a funny little man, isn't he?" Hannah mused as Ben opened the car door for her.

"Which one?"

"Well, Percy Lee, of course. He's already all enthusiastic about a meal that's a week away!"

"Yeah, funny, real funny," Ben repeated, deep in thought as he looked once more at the departing pair. Percy Lee might be as silly as any school boy and although he wasn't sure who Jess Newman was or wasn't, one thing he was certain about. Jess Newman was no man.

Back at the county jail the next morning, Deputy Ben Darling settled himself behind the desk while looking over a new batch of posters, telegrams and other notices that had come in recently from other counties. Sheriff Sam Allen was off to Webster County to testify in court in an assault case in which the prisoner had managed to win a change of venue from Laclede County. Cletus had gone upstairs to check on the four prisoners the county was holding including Willy Doolittle, the prisoner Ben had brought back from Dallas County earlier in the week.

"Everything good up there?" he called out, when he heard Cletus's boots clumping down the wooden stairs.

"Oh, yeah. Just fine, as long as you don't count Marvin Sparks' rantings. That one really is crazy. I know we have to wait for the judge to give the order but I won't mind at all when we can take him to the asylum over at Nevada."

Ben grinned. The mental cases always got to Cletus for some reason. Marvin didn't bother him to any great extent. Maybe because he had known Marvin's family all of his life, living as they did, not too far from Bennett Spring. And yes, he had always been a little bit crazy. Too many years of alcohol had certainly not helped.

"Hey, look at this. Did you know the bank at Rolla got robbed the other day?" Ben sat up straight while looking over a notice that included sketches of the suspected bank robbers.

"I heard something about it," Cletus answered, "but as always, it's somewhere else. Ain't like anything that exciting ever happens around here." He gave a casual glance to the notice Ben held out to him. The color drained from his face and his hands began to shake as he grasped the poster.

"Omigosh! Ben!"

"What is it? What's wrong?" Ben stood up next to Cletus, trying to discern what it was that his friend could see that he did not.

"This is the man! I saw him at the park, by your house. The other night!"

"Cletus, what are you talking about? The other night? At your uncle's farm?"

"No, no." Cletus shook his head and hit the picture of the suspects with his free hand.

"When I took the car over to my uncle's the first time, I found a feller down in the park. He'd just run into the new bridge with his car. I didn't think much about it at the time. I guess I didn't even mention it later because I didn't think it was any big thing. I mean, I was pretty tired and I helped pry his fender back—omigosh! I helped a bank robber just drive away!" He smacked his forehead with his palm. "What will Sheriff Sam say to that? Me helping fix a bank robber's car so he can drive off, happy as a pig in slop!"

Ben clapped his hands down on the distressed deputy's shoulders and guided him over to the chair by the desk. "Sit down and take it easy, Cletus," he consoled. "You didn't know who he was. What happened?"

Cletus spent the next few minutes filling in his friend on the events at the bridge that evening. Ben struggled to keep any trace of amusement from his face as Cletus shared his account.

"Man, I should have known something was up with this guy at the time. He was so...so...pleased with himself!" Cletus finally spit out.

"Well, I guess he was." Ben finally let a slight smile slide sideways across his face. "A deputy stops and instead of questioning or arresting him, helps him on his way. I'm sorry, Cletus, I know it ain't supposed to be funny, but in a way, it sorta is."

Cletus leaned forward, resting his head in his hands, his elbows on his knees. "Yeah, I guess it is. I hate to hear what the sheriff is going to say."

"Well, maybe it won't be so bad," Ben continued to try to console him. "After all, at least you can tell him that this feller has been spotted in the area and the sheriff can take it from there. What else can you remember about him? What was he wearing? Any idea where he was going? What kind of car was he driving? A plain one? A fancy one? Think, Cletus. The more information you can recall the more it will help and the less the sheriff is likely to think about the other part of it."

"What other part?"

"Umm, how one of his deputies let a bank robber walk away."

CHAPTER 6

Thursday. How could it be Thursday already? Jessica wondered as she crept out of the barracks before the first streaks of dawn washed across the eastern sky. Being part of the cooking crew had proved advantageous in that she was up and out of the barracks, and headed towards the dining hall long before all the others. It beat the alternative. She had tried to be one of the first up from the beginning. Otherwise, she found herself with her blanket pulled up over her head, while in the barracks, to make sure she didn't see what she shouldn't. The others teased that she was one extreme or the other, the earliest to rise or the last one out of her rack. At least today looked like it might finally be clear, she noticed as she glanced up at a starry sky. The rainy weather was playing havoc with their various work projects, throwing everything behind.

She stumbled on to the latrines. She tried to get in

and get out quickly before the others and it was definitely the place where she kept her eyes on her own boots. She had told Percy Lee she had guts that didn't work right and she was embarrassed about it. She explained that it meant that she had to go to the bathroom more often than most. It was Jesse's idea, a way to disguise why she went to the latrines and didn't step behind a tree like so many of the rest did to relieve themselves. Percy Lee suggested she might see the camp doctor but Jessica assured him she would be fine.

Jessica scooted inside the back door of the mess hall to find the place was already hopping, full of the noise of a busy kitchen, banging cookware, friendly banter, frying meat--ham this morning—and the loud voice of the head cook echoing over all.

"Top of the morning to you, Jess," Lt. Spuds Emerson called out as he cracked another egg into a huge bowl that already held several dozen. "Running a little behind are you this morning? Tough getting used to this new schedule of starting work at 5 am?"

"Yes, sir, sorry."

"You'll get there," he laughed. "You can start over there. Making hockey pucks this morning."

"Excuse me, sir?"

"Hockey pucks, kid. What? You don't play hockey?"

"No." It was her turn to smile. "Not enough ice down this way, most of the time."

"What a shame!" He shook his head. "What's a childhood without a good game of hockey now and then? You people did not grow up in Michigan, I can tell." He let out a loud guffaw and began to whip the eggs into a yellow froth.

Jessica was soon turning out pan after pan of warm tender biscuits. More than once she had complained when Grammy had insisted she learn to cook and bake. She preferred to be on the river with Jesse, working the horses with her father or doing anything else outside. For the first time she could remember, she was truly thankful she had learned the lessons in the kitchen that Grammy insisted would one day prove important.

She was standing in the mess line a short time later but on the serving side, forking a slice of fried ham on each passing tray.

"Hey, Jess," Percy Lee greeted her as he came through the line. "What's good today?"

"All of it, of course," she laughed as she answered back. "Eat up because after this, I get to go peel potatoes. A mountain of 'em."

"Sorry," he laughed. "I think it beats hauling and flipping rocks all day and that's what I'll be doing today."

"Well, you are right about that."

"You gonna be ready to go to supper tonight at that deputy's house? What was his name again?"

"Ben Darling," she answered as a cloud swept over her countenance.

"What's a-matter? You don't want to go?"

"Oh, no." She tried to back out of any more discussion of the upcoming visit to the Darling household. "It's no problem, really. I just—hey, you got to move along, Percy Lee. More folks waiting for breakfast. See you later."

"Yeah, yeah, okay." He moved on down the line and Jessica was grateful not to have to think about what was coming later in the day. She busied herself washing trays after breakfast and then started on the waiting mound of potatoes. She was soon joined by the lieutenant.

"I'll get somebody else over to help in a minute," he commented as he picked up a knife and started. We got those other two back from the infirmary. Wonder if they were really sick at all or just looking for a day or two of sleep."

Jessica snickered but didn't say anything. "So is your name really Spuds? Like potatoes?" she asked after a few minutes of silent peeling.

"Well, yeah," he smiled. "Real name is Stanley, just like my father, but the name never really fit me according to my mom.

"Let's see. Jess. You're the one they said took care of the horses that first day you came in, right?"

"Yes." She concentrated on the knife in her hand, peeling the potato in one long strip. It helped to make the boring task a bit more interesting.

"Do you have horses?"

"We used to, when I was growing up," she answered.

"Wow, I always thought it would be fun to own a horse."

The two continued to chat about their homes and what their future might hold.

"They send most of our money home, but that's good," Spuds commented. "A dollar a day adds up pretty good over time. My mom is using it, for her and my dad. He's pretty sick but she promised she would save a little back for me for when I get out so maybe with that I can get some tools and start working on cars."

"That would be good," Jessica mused.

"What do you want to do when you get out of here?" Spuds asked.

"Oh, goodness. I have no idea. I guess I'm thinking I just got here and it's enough to try and get used to that for now."

"Well, I've been here since the beginning, two years already," Spuds continued, "so I'm ready to start thinking about other things."

"Two whole years?"

"Yeah, kid. This is quite a project they got going here, building a park. You don't get that done in a month or two."

Jessica giggled. "I guess that's true."

"I started out just like this, peeling potatoes and then over time, they eventually put me in charge of the whole kitchen. It's been interesting to say the least, but I'm getting married in another few weeks so I'll be out of this man's outfit soon enough."

"Married? Going back home then?"

"No. Marrying a little gal from right here in Bennett Spring."

"Really?"

"Yeah, Mary Beth Chapman. She's Suzie's niece."

"Suzie?"

"Suzie. The lady that does the laundry down below."

"I don't guess I know…"

"What do you mean? Who does your laundry?"

"Well, nobody. I mean, I've just washed out a shirt when I need it, now and then."

Spuds shook his head with a grin as he went to work on another potato. "Kid, ain't it bad enough they got us cooking, peeling potatoes and such? How much women's work are you willing to do? Go find Suzie, down below where the rocks are all flat along the one side of the spring branch. She's down there most days, washing clothes for this outfit. She'll wash your clothes for you and she don't even charge that much."

Jessica thought about the fact that she was now in a position to pay someone else to do her laundry and a little smile crept across her face.

"What's so funny?" Spuds asked, trying to discern

her thoughts.

"Oh, nothing." Jessica covered her amusement by concentrating on the potato she was peeling. "So you met Mary Beth here?"

"Yeah, we met over at the church, at a dinner they had last summer. One thing led to another and I've decided to stay right here. I'm just from up the road a ways at Camdenton anyway so it's not that far to go see my folks. Going to be real different but I think it will be good. Her uncle has a shop working on cars and he says I can work with him. Her folks have a little cabin on their property and we're going to start out there."

"That will be nice for you both then," she added with a nod. "Congratulations."

"Well, thanks, Jess."

She was soon busy, boiling and mashing potatoes to go with canned Salisbury steaks and green beans for the midday meal. Once the noon time trays had been washed, she was finished with her dining hall chores for the day.

Back at the barracks, she sat on her bunk and looked over a handful of educational materials that had been left on her bed. It seems that life in the CCC also included schooling. She stretched out to read one of the booklets as a light rain began to tap softly on the roof. Most of this stuff looked pretty basic, she thought. She had always done well in school so it should be easy enough.

"Jess! Jess! Come on, wake up!" Percy Lee was

standing over her, shaking her by the shoulder.

Her eyes flew open wide as she tried to gauge her situation. She still held the education pamphlet in one hand.

"Come on, Jess. We'll be late to dinner at that deputy's house. We don't want to walk in when they're serving dinner. My ma always said that was a rude thing to do," Percy Lee spoke as he rubbed at his boots with a scrap of a rag in a vain attempt to clean them.

"Oh, yeah." She rolled over without enthusiasm and sat up, making sure not to hit her head on the above bunk as she had already done a couple of times. She ran her fingers through her short hair and pulled her cap down low over her eyes.

"Ready?" Percy Lee asked.

"Sure." They made their way out of the barracks, pushing past some of the others who were in various stages of coming in from the work day, catching a little rest and getting ready for dinner at the mess hall once again.

"Where you two off to?" one of the others called out. "Somebody said you got an invite to dinner?"

"That's right," Percy Lee hooted. "We're gonna eat real food while you fellers dig into more of the same at the mess hall. Eat your heart out!"

"Yeah, smart guys, are you?" Someone threw a balled up dirty sock.

"Hee, hee," Percy Lee chortled as he fended off the

LAURA L. VALENTI

harmless missile but stumbled into another man who was leaning over from his bunk while he unlaced his boots.

"Hey, watch it, kid!"

"Come on, Percy Lee." Jessica caught him by the upper arm and pushed him ahead of her out the door. "Don't aggravate them now."

"Why not?" Percy Lee still wore a wide grin. "Might as well, when you get the chance. They don't mind hassling us as the two smallest ones in the outfit or ain't you noticed that?"

"Hmpf," she snorted. "I noticed. But it ain't like we can do a whole lot about it. Just best to keep your head down and not give 'em anything more to use against us, if you know what I mean."

"Ain't no fun in that." His lopsided grin reminded her of a happy hound dog who had just been given a bone.

"Come on." She walked towards the spring and the Darling house, with Percy Lee trailing along behind. "So what've you been doing for work around here?"

"Right there." He turned around as they had just passed the triple-arched bridge. The naked concrete was partially covered with flat, sand-colored stone. "I'm hauling the stones from that stack, as Lt. John Kelly directs and we're covering that new bridge with 'em. They say we're going to cover the whole bridge before we're done. That'll look real nice, don't you think?"

"Yeah, it will." She looked back over her shoulder. "Lot of work though, huh?"

"Oh, you bet," Percy Lee agreed. "It ain't light work, that's for sure."

They strolled along the spring branch, close to the water's edge. "Man, that water is cold." Percy Lee gave an exaggerated shudder.

"Spring water," Jessica answered. "It's not so bad, if'n you're used to it."

"You think?" He shook again, this time like a dog shaking water from its coat. "I'm not much of a swimmer. We always played around in an old swimming hole back home, but it wasn't very deep and it was lots warmer water than this. You swim?"

"Oh, yes." Her eyes shone. "All the time. The Eleven Point is an all spring-fed big river. My papa used to guide city folks on fishing trips once in awhile to go fishing for three or four days at a time." They passed by Jessica's secret bathing spot, without speaking. She thought she would be looking to get back there soon.

"Really? How does that work?"

"Well, we're talking before money all got so tight and all but they'd come from the city, men mostly, and my papa would get the supplies and flat-bottomed boats all ready for them and then take 'em up river. Then they'd float back down to Riverton. My brother would get to go along more often than me but I got to go one time."

"Wow, spend three or four days on the river at

once? I don't know if I'd like that or not."

"Oh, it was great," she answered with enthusiasm. "Fishing and swimming the whole way."

Percy Lee gave another exaggerated shiver in disagreement.

As they approached the spring itself, they saw two trout fishermen, casting their lines. In the rays of a slanting afternoon sun, their golden silhouettes shone as they gracefully let their lines float in a long leisurely fashion before delicately dropping their dry flies exactly where they wanted them. A few seconds hesitation and the flies on the end of the lines flew again and again. The young workers stood stock still, not wanting to disturb the exquisite scene before them, until the fishermen's rhythm was broken by the leap of a rainbow trout above the gleaming surface of the water.

"There you go!" The taller one stopped to admire the fish on the other's line.

Jessica recognized Ben Darling's voice. She and Percy Lee drew closer as the blond man removed the fish from his line and tucked it into the creel basket he wore at his waist.

"Hello," Jessica said shyly and the two fishermen turned towards her.

"Hello, yourself." Ben looked up without smiling. "J.C., these are the two CCC fellers Ma invited to dinner tonight, Jess and Percy Lee. This is J.C. Shine, my brother-in-law."

"Nice to meet you," Jessica answered with a wave

as she stood on dry ground and J.C. and Ben remained standing in hip deep water in their waders.

"The others are up at the house," Ben continued. "We'll be along in a few minutes. We thought we'd get in a little fishing before supper."

"We'll see you up there." Despite her words, Jessica lingered, watching the agile movements of the two anglers.

"That was real fine, seeing them fish like that, huh?" Percy Lee was equally impressed as their steps turned on past the spring towards the Darling house.

"Oh yes." Jessica was almost breathless. "It is truly beautiful. I like to fish but it never looks nothing like that."

At the Darling house, they were quickly welcomed inside where they met Becky. Esther was thrilled to see Jessica again and was still full of questions for her and now her companion, Percy Lee.

Dinner was a rollicking gabfest as conversation seemed to go in as many directions as there were people at the table, which included the entire Darling family as well as the two CCC recruits. Fried chicken, home-canned beets, lettuce and spinach salad, mashed potatoes and gravy filled their plates. After the last couple of days she'd spent peeling potatoes, Jessica wasn't sure she could bear the sight of more potatoes, but Hannah Darling's potatoes mixed with real butter and fresh milk were beyond compare and she enjoyed the entire meal.

Percy Lee and Esther ended up in a giggly conversation about her milk cows and Percy Lee told her he would like to see her very special cows.

"Go and see the cows, then," Hannah told them, "while Becky and I clear away some of these dishes. We'll have some chocolate cake a little later but right now..." She cast a cautious eye towards Zeb and J.C. who had gotten into a long political conversation as they picked up yesterday's newspaper to check a story there.

"Jess, you and Ben don't have to listen to their nonsense," Hannah muttered under her breath.

"Come on," Ben said. "We'll go outside for a minute."

Jessica followed him to a couple of chairs on the front porch. An old hound, all gray around his muzzle, lay at the far end of the porch and thumped his tail on the wooden floor as they approached.

"Hey, Homer." Ben sat down closest to the dog and rubbed his ears.

"He's a really old dog," Jessica observed.

"Yeah, about thirteen or so these days," Ben said. "Getting up there in years, he is."

Jessica nodded and said nothing.

"So, how's the CCC life treating you so far?"

"Oh, fine. I got no complaints."

"I see," he glanced sideways at her for a brief moment. "So what are you doing exactly?"

"Uh, well." She wondered briefly, if he was just making conversation or if he was really looking for information. "I've been making mortar for some of the stone work and the last couple of the days, I've been cooking."

"Cooking?" he sounded surprised.

"Yeah, working in the kitchen, making biscuits, peeling potatoes and washing dinner trays and the like."

"I see," he repeated. He dropped his hand from the dog's ears and leaned forward but kept his eyes trained on her.

"So that was your brother here the other night?" Jessica thought she better say something to direct the conversation away from herself. "How is he doing? He looked like he'd had quite the rough trip from Oklahoma."

"Yeah, well, a rough trip. That kind of describes Jake's whole life," he added as he ran his hand through his sandy curls. "He don't seem to know how to make life easy on himself."

"What do you mean?"

"He stayed here a day or two with the folks but he's already gone back up with that bunch on Poker Ridge. No sense at all. He got in trouble with them years ago and then went to Oklahoma a couple of years ago with somebody who promised him work and well, never mind..." He cut himself off and switched back to his original focus.

"Jess...or whatever your name is, I know you are

not who or what you're claiming to be down there at the CCC camp. Now I don't pretend to know exactly what you're up to, but in my line of work what you're doing is usually called fraud, pretending to be something you're not."

Her eyes widened as his words rolled on but she didn't hear most of what he said after that as her head began to spin. Here it is, her mind raced. He's the law and he's going to haul me off to jail. She wanted to jump up and run, but she could feel her knees had already turned to jelly. Of all the ways she had imagined in her nightmares she might be turned out, she had never imagined it would happen at the end of a fine meal in a comfy home.

"...and I got to say, I don't appreciate you up here basically lying to my family as well, getting them involved in whatever shenanigans you might be wrapped up in."

"This ain't no fraud." She finally found her voice. "It's not like that and I never meant to get your family mixed up in it neither. I came here with some horses, remember? And then I got invited back for today and if you remember, I didn't exactly jump at that chance either." She sounded like such a whiney little girl, she thought to herself, which made her hate the whole situation even more.

"Then how is it?" Ben tried to sound more demanding than he felt. The truth is the more time he spent around her, the harder it was to think of her as anything but a lovely young girl. Despite her ill-fitting green uniform and that silly worn gray army cap she wore, she had a grace and an ease about her that he found quite charming.

"Do you even know what fraud is?"

"Well, yes, it's like when you sign somebody else's name, to steal money or something," she stammered while wondering if she really could be accused of that. She recalled Jesse's words…either one of us could rightfully claim to be Jess Newman.

"Yes, or pretending to be something you're not to get money out of someone else," he added.

"I know…" She hesitated. "I'm not sure what you're talking about exactly." How could he really know anything? She began to grapple for answers.

"I know you ain't no feller." Ben leveled his gaze on her.

"Who told you that?" was all she could think to ask.

"Nobody that you know," he countered. "But I have it on excellent authority."

Jessica sat silently, staring at the floor boards beneath her feet.

"Look," she began, not even certain as to where she was going yet. "It's not what you say. It's not any kind of fraud, I swear. My name is Jess Newman. That's not a lie. It won't be long, Deputy, I promise, that I'll be here, that is. If you can give me a little more time. I ain't doing nothing wrong, not really. I'm working real hard. The CCC is getting their money's worth but there are others involved and if I tell you more than that, then they'll be hurt, too—"

"There are others? Other girls pretending to be—"

"No, not like that." Jessica quickly corrected his misconception.

"No one here that you might see," she sighed heavily. "I really can't say more because if I do, innocent people are going to suffer. No one here knows. I haven't told a soul and that's why I don't know how it is that you know…"

"Well, never you mind that part of it." He thought with more than a bit of shame of the night he had stumbled upon her, bathing in solitude. He had no intention of revealing to her how he had discovered the truth. "I do know and I haven't told anyone either…yet. But I'm a law officer and if there is any kind of trickery or illegality going on here, I can't sit still and not do anything about it."

"I promise you, by all that is and all that I know," Jessica looked him in the eye and laid her right hand over her heart, "there isn't. It's just a bad situation that will be taken care of very soon, a few weeks, no more."

"Well, then…"

Percy Lee and Esther ran up the path from the barn. "Hey, she's pretty fast," Percy Lee laughed as he scooted up behind the giggling Esther.

"So how were the cows, Sprig?" Ben asked while still watching Jessica, whose eyes were once again trained on her own boots.

She wiped the back of her hand across her eyes. How would she explain to the others why she was sitting here so nice and quiet with Ben Darling and crying like a baby?

"Hey, Jess, you should see 'em," Percy Lee went on, oblivious to her situation. "Esther here has got a couple of good-looking cows down there and chickens and—"

"I've seen cows before, Percy Lee. Thanks just the same," she muttered. "I'll be back." Jessica stood up and walked down the path towards the outhouse. Once inside, she simply leaned up against the door and let her tears flow. How did Jesse really think she could ever pull this off? Now the jig was up and she would soon end up in jail. She wondered idly how long she might have to sit there before Jesse would get here and rescue her.

After a few minutes, she took a deep breath and began to pull herself together. Once outside, she could see Esther was the only one still on the porch. "Come on, Jess," the little one called. "We got chocolate cake and Ma says we got to wait for you since you're company."

That brought a weak smile to her face despite her mood.

CHAPTER 7

Two mornings later, Jessica was peeling potatoes once again when Captain Smith stuck his head in the kitchen. "Newman!" he called and she jumped as she had been wool-gathering about jail and what might become of her after that.

"Yes, sir," she managed to answer as she slipped off her stool.

"Had enough kitchen work for awhile? Hope so, because I need your help elsewhere. They're back up to full crew in here, so come on with you."

"Yes sir," she answered again and stripped off her apron. "See ya, Spuds," Jessica waved as she followed the captain out of the mess hall.

"Hop in," he called from the driver's seat of an army Jeep.

They were soon moving up a long hill, out of the park area and then just as quickly, they took a sharp left turn and headed back towards a little brown house tucked in the woods, overlooking the church, the nearby fields, and the last remains of the village of Brice. The exploding greenery, the one thing that had benefitted enormously from the damp rainy weather, made it impossible to see the valley below and all but hid the house from view.

"That's where J.C. Shine lives," Captain Smith began to explain as he slowed the Jeep, "and this is the problem." He stopped the Jeep as they came up to a huge tree that lay across the road which formed a large circle in front of the house.

"Shine is the newspaper editor in town."

"Yes, sir. He was at Mrs. Darling's house the other night. The lady who invited me and Percy Lee to dinner."

"Oh, that's right. I forgot he's married into the Darling family. I swear, these people are all related one way or another around here."

Jessica grinned at the captain. "Where are you from, sir? If'n you don't mind me asking."

"St. Louis," he answered. "And yes, it's quite a bit different than here. Anyway, J.C. Shine had lunch a couple days ago with my boss at some Chamber of Commerce deal. Shine tells him about this tree that fell across his road and how he needs it out of there and the next thing you know, the boss volunteers us to take care of it. A little community cooperation he calls it. Now I can get some boys up here with a crosscut saw to cut it up but I don't have enough trucks to do what we're trying to do down below as is. I certainly don't have a truck I can spare for the likes of firewood and I don't want to mess with the wood anyway. That's somebody else's headache. So here's what I'm wanting to know. If we manage to borrow those draft horses again from that farmer, can you get this out of here with them if we get it cut up in a couple of pieces?"

"Oh, sure." Jessica was glad to know where he was going with all this explanation. "Shouldn't be a problem." She climbed out of the Jeep and stepped over to take a closer look at the tree. It was huge and apparently had simply fallen over due to the softened soil after so much rain. She took a step closer to get a better look at the partially-rotted root ball that stood as high as she was tall.

"Okay, let's do this then," the captain continued. "I've got a meeting with the CCC superintendent and I'm headed there now. I'll tell him we'll take care of Mr. Shine's problem. You go over to the house and let Mrs. Shine know, will you? They tell me there's a path down the back of the hillside over there that'll bring you out just above the hatchery. You head that way and I'll see what we have to do to make arrangements with that farmer to borrow his horses. I've heard through the grapevine that the local folks think one of our boys did a good job of taking care of those horses after the accident—that would be you, so that should work in our favor. If he doesn't want to lend the horses directly, maybe he'll come help us out and take care of it himself. I really don't care, as long as we get it out of here and I don't have to give up one of our trucks to do it."

"Yes, sir," Jessica answered and stayed by the fallen

tree as the captain turned the Jeep around and headed back the way they had come.

Jessica knocked on the door of the little brown house, happy at the thought of seeing the very friendly Becky Shine once again. No answer came in response to her second or third knock. For some reason, she dared to twist the glass doorknob and call out.

"Mrs. Shine. Becky Shine, are you here? It's Jess Newman." She took a step inside the tiny vestibule and called out again.

A low moan could be heard from somewhere in the back of the house. Jessica couldn't be sure but it was enough to start her moving through the small living room and around the corner down the hall.

"Mrs. Shine?" She pushed open a door to her left and scurried down the long flight of wooden steps when she saw Becky Shine, lying on the platform at the bottom of the stairs.

"Mrs. Shine! Oh my lands! What happened? Can you get up?" Jessica reached under the woman's arms to help pull her to a seated position.

"Oh, Jess," Becky leaned her head on Jessica's shoulder. "I'm so glad you're here. Can you help get me up the stairs to the bed? I'm afraid I might be in real trouble here."

"Of course. Here." Jessica slipped Becky's arm around her neck and lifted her to her feet, with her own arm around Becky's ample waist. Together, they made their way, slow and steady, up the stairs.

"Take it easy, not too fast," Jessica cautioned.

"Oh, Jess." Becky doubled over in pain, pulling her free arm across her belly before they reached the top step.

"It's okay." Jessica stopped and waited. She glanced back over her shoulder and saw a trail of blood and water behind them. "Mrs. Shine—"

"Becky. Just call me Becky," she panted softly.

"Miz Becky, then," Jessica tried again. "We got to get you to that bed. Come on."

They struggled into the hallway and then a quick left into the bedroom. Jessica threw back the covers and gently eased the pregnant woman down onto the sheets.

"Help me, here," Becky instructed as she began to struggle out of her clothes.

"Miz Becky…I..uh," Jessica wasn't sure what she should do next.

"Look," Becky was nearly breathless but still all business. "I'm sorry but I don't know how to say this politely so I'm just going to spit it out. I know the truth. I mean, you may be in the CCC at the moment but you are no young man. What's your real name? Jessie? Jessica?"

"Jessica," she answered in a voice that was barely a whisper.

"Well, Jessica then." She took in a quick breath through gritted teeth. "We've got our hands full here for the moment. I know how to deliver babies.

I've done it many times in this valley in the last few years but it never occurred to me that I might have to deliver my own."

"Miz Becky, how can you possibly…" Jessica stammered as the realization began to dawn.

"I can't, to be honest, but you can. I'll help you. You'll need to listen and work with me and together, we're going to make sure these little ones come into the world just fine."

"You talked about it at dinner the other night. The doctor told you last week you're having twins! Oh, Miz Becky…."

"Now, Jessica, come on. Pull yourself together. I'm the one who is supposed to be in a panic about now." She struggled to push herself into a semi-sitting position in the bed and Jessica hurriedly reached around to position pillows behind her. In the kitchen and then the bathroom, Jessica rounded up dishtowels and towels as per Becky's instructions.

"But Miz Becky, have you got a telephone? I could call someone—"

"Well, that would be nice, if I had a phone that worked when it rained. That's a problem with all the phones around here at Bennett Spring. They all go out when it rains very much. I tried to go down those steps earlier because of the water. J.C.'s been worried because we've actually had flooding in the basement and I thought I'd check on it and well, you see how that turned out. Not so smart on my part."

"How long were you down there on the floor?"

"Oh, I don't really know." She laid the back of her wrist across her forehead. "I was thinking about the chicken and rice soup I'd made for lunch and then I thought I'd just scoot downstairs and take a look…" She closed her eyes and looked almost as if she might sleep but the moment passed and she tensed again.

"Maybe I should try going down the hill to get help…" Jessica tried again.

"Jessica, please." Becky reached out and took her hand. "I can be pretty brave in all of this if I have to, but I don't want you to go. Please don't leave me."

"Okay, okay." Jessica took a deep breath and made a decision. "I'll stay here with you. Tell me what I need to do and I'll do it."

A weak but definitive smile crossed Becky's face. "Have you ever seen a baby born before?"

Jessica shook her head. "Only horses and cows. They come out in a sack and sort of hit the ground and are on their feet pretty quick."

Becky shook her head with a smile. "Well, don't expect these little ones to be up walking around that quick. Takes quite a bit longer, too. Most of the time. Sometimes, not." She reached and patted Jessica's hand. "Thanks for staying. I've been thinking. J.C. told me he planned to come home early today so that should help. He was supposed to talk to somebody about that tree down across the drive out front."

"Oh, that would be me. Or more likely the captain. That's why I was here. The captain wanted me to look and see if I could move the tree with horses once they cut it, rather than cutting it small enough to load in a truck."

Becky stared at her for a moment, uncomprehending and then she began to laugh. "Well, that's a different twist on things." The statement ended in a hiss. "Talk to me, Jessica. Tell me something, anything. What do you do for the CCC? How did you ever get into the CCC as a girl?"

"Can I ask you something first?"

"Sure."

"How did you find out about me? Did I do something or say something to give it away?"

Becky grinned. "Little brothers still talk to their big sisters when they have problems they can't figure out. Benji. Sorry. Ben. He told me, or I should say, he asked me what to do about you, about the situation." She chuckled. "For whatever reason, you've managed to turn my brother inside out over this."

"Ma'am?"

"He told me you wouldn't tell him why you were here or how you got here and that really got to him for some reason."

"Well, he wouldn't tell me how he found

out…about me, I mean. I know nobody here told him, but he knew!"

"Oh, Jessica." Becky laughed again despite the labor pains. "You two are quite the pair! If I tell you how he found out, will you tell me how you ended up in the CCC?"

"Yes, I will!" Jessica's eyes unexpectedly filled with tears. "I want so badly to talk to someone about all of this. It has been so awful and so lonely."

"Well, talk to me then." Becky gave another painful gasp. She patted the side of the bed for Jessica to sit down. "Tell me this story because I have a feeling it has got to be a good one!"

And so the two women talked and laughed and cried and sipped a little soup together. By the end of the afternoon there were screams of pain and then of joy as a baby boy appeared. Becky had spoken the truth. She knew exactly what had to be done, when and how. Directing Jessica kept her focused and when she wanted to give up and simply be a patient, she concentrated on the younger woman and how hard she was trying to do everything that was asked of her. Jessica cleaned the baby's mouth and nose, turned him upside down briefly and rejoiced and gave thanks as he opened his mouth and gave a lusty wail. Becky relaxed and collapsed back against the pillows as Jessica quickly wrapped the new baby in a towel and laid him in his mother's arms.

Jessica wiped the back of her hand across her

forehead and fell as much as sat in the overstuffed chair next to the bed. They looked so lovely, so peaceful together. The charmed moment did not last long as Becky convulsed again and doubled up as the pain returned. Jessica scooped up the baby as Becky strained. She turned and placed the baby gently in the upholstered chair where she had been sitting.

"Here we go again." Becky tried to make a joke but it ended in a grimace and a moan.

"You can do this," Jessica encouraged. "Look at that beautiful baby boy over there. There's another one waiting in the wings now and we've got to get him or maybe it's a her. Wouldn't that be fun? Like me and Jesse. But whichever, we've got to get him out, too. I know you can do this. Please, Becky."

Becky Shine opened her eyes as another wave of pain engulfed her. "All right," she whispered. "One more time."

"Thanks so much for the ride home, Ben." J.C. Shine occupied the passenger seat of the deputy's car as they made the turn onto the road leading to the park entrance. "I told Becky I was going to get home early today and instead, well, I couldn't believe it when my car wouldn't even start there at the office this afternoon. Glad you were available. The mechanic said he could have my car ready tomorrow but I didn't want to leave Becky alone another night this week. I've been doing way too much of that lately. And now that the doctor has told us twins are on the way…" He shook his head. "And of course, these crazy phones don't work well in the rain so I couldn't even call her to tell her."

"It's no problem. I never mind an excuse to come home for a night. I've been worried about Becky anyway. She's looking pretty tired these days."

"I know. I asked your mother but she assures me it's just the end of her time and that once the babies are born, she'll be better until she gets even more tired taking care of them but then, that too will pass in a few months. Sounds like we're all going to be busy and with very little sleep over the course of the next many days," J.C. added with a short laugh.

"Well, count on me to come and sleep on your couch now and then," Ben laughed. "I remember quite a bit about taking care of Esther when she was little. Not an expert or anything but I can do my part to help out."

"Hey, I'm not too proud to take you up on that! I may have printer's ink running through my veins these days but what I don't know about diapers and Pablum boggles the mind."

And with that, J.C. changed the subject as they pulled into his drive. "Hey, did I show you that new fly I got from the retired typesetter at the newspaper? He stopped by one day last week and he was talking about how fortunate I was to live at Bennett Spring. He gave me this little mayfly he had tied. If you've got an extra minute, come on in and I'll show it to you."

"Sure." Ben parked the car and followed his

brother-in-law into his house.

"Becky?" J.C. called as they tromped into the living room. "Becky? Are you here?"

"Back here," came a voice from the bedroom he didn't recognize.

"Glory to Heaven." J.C.'s voice dropped to a prayer as he found his wife in the bed cradling his new daughter and a CCC recruit, in a bloody apron, holding his baby son.

"Jess?" Ben was right behind J.C. "What's going on?"

Jessica looked up with a tired smile on her face. "I came here to see about cutting up a tree and instead I…well, we've been a little busy this afternoon."

"I'd say you have," J.C. continued to speak in a voice husky with emotion. "Becky, are you…are you all right?" He dropped to his knees beside the bed.

The exhausted woman opened her eyes wearily. "Hi, sweetheart," she managed to say. "Meet your new son and your new daughter. And my new friend, Jessica."

"Jessica, is it?" J.C. laughed as a quizzical expression crossed his face. "Nice to meet you, Jessica." She handed him the baby she had been holding.

Ben stood at the bedroom door, surveying the wondrous scene of his niece and nephew's arrival. "But how did you end up here?" He was still trying to sort out Jess Newman's part in all of it.

"It's kinda crazy." Jessica began to untie the apron at her neck. "What time is it? I better get back to the camp. Captain Smith will be wonderin' what's become of me. I was supposed to meet up with him about the horses and moving that tree and—"

"That downed tree? That's how you ended up here?" J.C.'s brow creased in a frown as he tried to follow the fractured conversation.

"Yes, I came up to see about the tree and then to tell Becky, I mean Mrs. Shine, what the captain decided and then I found her at the bottom of the steps and then...." Her breathless explanation turned to a lump in her throat that threatened to overwhelm her. She pushed past Ben and ran towards the kitchen.

"Jess. Wait." Ben turned to follow.

"Benji. Come back, please." Becky's voice was weak with fatigue but the urgency was no less evident. "Don't you bother that girl, do you hear me? It's been a long afternoon and we have two new babies to show for it but I also learned a lot about her. I'm too tired to tell it all to you now, but I'll tell you this. It will all be taken care of very soon. She's doing the best she can for now. Don't make things any harder for her, you hear?"

"I hear you," he grinned. "And if you say so, then I can live with that. A boy and a girl, heh? Well, God bless you, Becky, it don't get much better than that!" He laughed out loud and slapped J.C. on the back as he headed towards the kitchen.

"Becky, are you all right? Are they all right? What do I need to do to help?" J.C.'s voice faded behind him as Ben walked away. He had a lot to learn, Ben thought to himself.

Approaching Jessica from behind, Ben asked gently, "Is everything under control in here?" He handed her a clean towel as she finished rinsing her face and washing her hands at the kitchen sink.

"Yeah, I guess so." She let a deep sigh escape. "It's been pretty overwhelming. I've never done anything like this before. When my little sister was born, I went to a neighbor's house. I never imagined…" She stopped speaking and looked down at her green uniform that was now stained here and there, despite the apron that Becky had suggested at one point. "Oh my! How am I going to explain this down below?"

"Hmm. I say we get you something from Becky's closet and we'll get your uniform washed before you wear it back to work. Tell your captain where you've been but I wouldn't tell any of the rest of those fellers. It might get them to thinking in directions you don't want them to go right now."

"Pardon?" She looked up in confusion.

"If they have any idea as to your real…what should I say? Your real identity, uh…this could get them thinking about it a little too much."

"Oh, you're right." She smiled in spite of her situation. "It's like when I got your sister up to the bed today and she started taking off her things. All I could think was, now what am I supposed to do about this? No boy would stand still for that." She laughed and covered her face in exhaustion and embarrassment. "We never imagined how complicated this could become."

"We?"

"My brother, Jesse, and me. He's the one who is really in the CCC, not me."

"Jesse? Jess?"

"Jesse and Jessica. My twin brother and me. I told you the truth. My name really is Jess Newman."

"Your twin brother. Well, you don't say. And where is he?"

"Still in Riverton, with a broken leg. He was in a bad accident the week before he was to come and he was afraid he might lose his place if he didn't show up, so I came instead. It's just for a few weeks. He ought to be along soon. I wrote to him and I've been waiting days now for a letter from him."

"Now that is starting to make some sense. Not a lot but…" He shook his head with a smile, in spite of himself. "But why didn't you just—"

"Just what? Wait?" She stiffened slightly. "We were afraid to take the chance. We're not the only ones, you know. We've got my grandma and my little brother and sister, Gabe and Grace, who are only eight and five. There's no work in Riverton. My dad went to St. Louis last year but he got TB and died. There's no money and we just…we couldn't wait." She stopped speaking and gave him a look that said more than any words.

"It's all right, honest. I'm not accusing anybody." Ben put his hands up in front of him as if to fend off an invisible attack. "I don't understand but it sounds like you do so if it's that important, I'm not going to interfere. You said it's going to be taken care of soon, right?"

"Yes." She bobbed her head.

"All right then," he agreed. "Let's see what we can do about getting you some clean duds. You want to get a bath before you go back?"

"You mean a real bath with warm water?" Her tired eyes widened at the thought of it.

"Yes, a real bath!" Ben Darling laughed so loud at her expression that J.C.'s head popped out the bedroom door down the hall.

"Everything all right in there?"

"Yes, yes, everything's fine," Ben assured him. "Tell Becky, Jessica needs to borrow some clothes and her bathroom for a little while."

CHAPTER 8

While Jessica enjoyed a hot bath, Ben made a quick trip across the valley. The Darling household was thrilled to hear the news but it was no small feat to convince Esther she should wait until the next day to meet her new tiny relatives. Zeb assured Hannah that he and Esther would be fine for the night and that she should go with Ben and spend the night at Becky's house.

"So you are our new midwife-in-training, heh?" Hannah greeted Jessica when she came out of the bathroom with her hair wrapped in a towel. Hannah cradled her grandson while J.C. held her granddaughter. "Becky told me the two of you had quite a day and here's the proof."

"Yes, we did," Jessica replied with a shy smile. "Is Becky all right? I mean, she is going to be fine, isn't she? I wasn't sure about so much of what had to be done but she told me exactly what to do and when. I guess I'm still worried about her."

"She's sleeping now." Hannah nodded as she rocked back and forth while seated in a wooden rocking chair in the living room. "She's really tired, of course, but I think she'll be fine. Maybe we'll get the doctor to come out here tomorrow or at the very least, Miz Darcey to make sure."

"That would be good," Jessica replied. "I guess I better get my hair combed and get back down the hill."

"Jess. Or I should say, Jessica. You don't have to go back, if you don't want to. This family owes you a tremendous debt. I am so grateful to the good Lord that you were here today. If you want to stay with us until you can get things worked out, you are more than welcome. Whatever you need."

"Oh, thank you, Mrs. Darling. That is so kind of you." She sat down on the settee, opposite the new grandmother. "I so appreciate that, but you all have already been so kind. I'm glad I was here today and could help but I've got to go back, to do what I promised. To do what I need to do to take care of my family."

"I understand. You are a strong young woman, Jessica. Your family should be proud."

"Thank you, ma'am." Jessica blushed and pulled the towel from her head. Her curls were starting to grow back from the short haircut that Jesse had given her weeks before.

"I'll bring your uniform back to you tomorrow, if that's all right with you," Hannah told her. "I'll get it washed yet tonight. I doubt there will be much sleeping going on here tonight," she giggled. "It should be dry tomorrow sometime. And in the meantime, when you're ready to get a bath again, don't be tripping around that spring branch in the dark. You come up here and visit these babies you helped bring into the world and get you a proper bath in warm water, you hear?"

"Yes, ma'am. I'll do that." Jessica's smile spread wide across her face and she felt herself relax more than she had since leaving home weeks before.

"Ben!" Hannah called to her son who had wandered into the kitchen while chatting with J.C. "Are you going to give this worker a ride back to the CCC barracks?"

Ben took Jessica down the hill and together, they found Captain Smith at work in his office, in the officers' barracks building.

"I was starting to wonder about you." The captain rubbed his chin while taking a long look at Jess Newman, now dressed in civilian garb. She had deliberately chosen one of J.C.'s worn shirts and an old pair of dungarees that had belonged to Becky. She hoped they would help her to continue her disguise but the way the captain was looking her over, once again, made her more nervous than ever.

"So you know how to deliver babies, too?" The captain raised an eyebrow in her direction.

"No, I don't. I helped deliver a foal a couple of times, years back. Mrs. Shine is a midwife and she

132

asked me to stay and help her. And she told me what to do. I wouldn't have done it but there wasn't anyone else and the phone was out." She looked down and shrugged. "I'm sorry if it made trouble here."

"Nah." He leaned back in his office chair. "No problem here. You're right about the phones. I found that out again today. I swear all it does is rain and then the phones don't work. How do you people get anything done around here?" he asked in exasperation as he grinned at Ben Darling, robbing his words of any offense.

"Get on back to your barracks for now, Newman. Did you get anything to eat?"

"Uh..." She glanced over her shoulder at Ben. "No, I really didn't but..."

"Omigosh, Jess. I'm sorry," Ben blurted out. "With all the excitement at Becky's, I never thought—"

"It's all right, really. I wasn't thinking about food either the last few hours." She gave him a winning smile and his heart leapt unexpectedly.

Captain Wilbur Smith's eyes darted back and forth between the two who stood in front of his desk. "Stop by the mess hall and see what you can scrounge up there," he instructed. "I'd say you've done your fair share towards contributing to good community relations today." A half smile creased his face as he watched Jessica walk away. He turned towards Ben . "So you've got what? A new niece and a new nephew. Quite a day for your family."

"Yeah, you could say that. Thanks for not coming down too hard on that kid. Jess was a real help today. I appreciate that."

"Not a problem." The captain's head was already back into his figures as he returned to his paperwork. "Thanks for getting him back to us. I was wondering. I hate the ones who run off, you know. There's not too many of them but it's one more headache. At least I don't have to go look for them like the military, but it just leaves us even more short-handed."

"Well, I don't think you have to worry about that one. Pretty dedicated as far as I can tell."

"You think?"

"Oh, yes, I think so," Ben Darling answered, as he thought about the offer his mother had made to Recruit Jess Newman earlier that evening.

Back in the barracks, Jessica collapsed onto her bunk, exhausted.

"Where you been all day and night?" Percy Lee whispered loudly as she fell into bed.

"Up at Miz Becky's house, on the hill," she answered, her face half in the pillow.

"Whatcha been doing up there all this time?"

"You wouldn't believe me, if'n I told you."

"Oh yeah. Try me." He propped himself up on one elbow to look over at her.

She rolled over on her back and sighed. "Not tonight. I am beat and I ain't even sure what I got to do tomorrow, work in the kitchen, drag a tree out of the road using horses—dang! I forgot to ask the captain about that."

"About what?"

"That's why I was up at Miz Becky's in the first place. A tree fell across their road and the captain agreed to get it out of there. Well, really, he didn't, but never mind. Anyway, he wants to use horses rather than a truck 'cause he says he doesn't have enough trucks and then I told him I could do it and…" Her voice drifted off.

Percy Lee grinned as he lay back down on his bunk. He had never seen anybody so tired that they fell asleep in the middle of an explanation.

With no further direction from the captain, Jessica returned to the kitchen the next morning to help with breakfast. After another day of cooking and tray washing, she was glad to escape the confines of the mess hall. Today, the sun was finally shining and she enjoyed the warm breeze as she walked across the field towards the old mill. Ox eye daisies and other wild flowers waved their bright faces in the light summer wind, seeming to enjoy the break from the rainy weather as much as she did.

"Hey, Jess!" She heard Percy Lee's voice call out as she got close to the mill. "Come look at this!" He was standing inside, up on the first floor of the mill.

"What are you doing up there?" she asked as she found her way to the door and scrambled inside to catch up to him.

"Helping. Are you ready? Wait 'til you see this!"

One of the men she had seen working at the trout hatchery was inside, loading something into the hopper for the mill.

"This here is Chester," Percy Lee made the introductions. "He works here at the fish hatchery and he gets to feed the fish every day. Now that would be a pretty good job, don't you think?"

"Hi," Jessica greeted him shyly.

Chester just smiled and continued to work as he shook his head at Percy Lee's antics.

"What's that smell?" Jessica wrinkled up her nose.

"Liver," Percy Lee laughed. "Look here. They cook all this stuff together, liver and soybeans and such and then grind it all up to feed them trout. Can you believe that?"

She followed Percy Lee around as he pointed out exactly what was being done.

"Ready?" Chester asked.

"Sure!" Percy Lee sang out.

Chester flipped the switch high on the wall and the sleeping mill came to life with a low rumble that quickly set the whole place to shaking with the turn of the turbine and the spinning of the many belts that extended one floor to the next. Jessica suddenly remembered being in Turner's Mill along the Eleven Point as a child with her father. How the noise and quaking had terrified her! Now it was still disconcerting but not the heart stopping fear she remembered. Still, when she turned and collided with Deputy Ben Darling she was more than a little taken aback. Over the noise of the mill, she had not heard him come in.

After a few moments, Chester shut off the machinery and the momentary silence was almost as deafening.

She stepped out on the large receiving dock at the back of the mill and the deputy followed. "What are you doing here?" she asked in surprise.

"Well, after all the excitement at our house and Becky's last night, I decided to take the day off," he grinned sheepishly. "The phones were finally working again so I called the sheriff and told him and he said that was fine. He said to stay out here today because in the morning he needs me to go meet a transport at the Dallas County line anyway. Ma was so excited about everything, she even let Esther stay home from school today and go spend the day with her and Becky and the new little ones. That's pretty impressive because Ma never let any of us play hooky for nothing!"

"Well, good. I'm glad for Esther. She probably felt kind of left out of things last night," Jessica added.

Percy Lee tumbled out of the mill, behind them. "Well, what do you think of that?"

"Pretty noisy, like all mills, I guess." Jessica smiled at his obvious enthusiasm over the entire process. "I remember the mill upriver at home when I was little but I always found it pretty scary. So noisy with the floor about shaking right out from under you."

"Yeah, but that's the really great part of it!" Percy Lee went on. "I'm helping Chester with the feed and afterwards he's going to take me down and show me how to feed the fish. See ya later, Jess!" And with that, he ducked back inside.

"Do you have to go back to work, too?" Ben asked.

"No. I've been feeding men today, not fish, which means I start early but I get done early, too. They told me the captain was at the new picnic shelter they're building up by the spring. I was thinking of walking over there and checking with him to see what he decided about the horses and the downed tree up at Becky's house."

"Well, I would offer you a ride but I walked down from Becky's house. I left the car up there because since J.C. didn't go to work today he still doesn't have a car either. Pa brought Esther by early this morning and with her and Ma and Becky there, they didn't need me underfoot, too. J.C., he's up there learning how to be a dad, I think, or maybe just getting some extra shut eye. There wasn't much sleeping going on in that house last night, I can tell you," he added with a laugh.

"I bet that's true," Becky smiled in return. "It's a beautiful afternoon and I was looking forward to the walk anyway."

"Would you like some company?" he asked as he followed her down the steps of the mill.

"I guess that would be all right." She gave him a

sideways glance. "So what does that mean, to meet a transport, in the morning?"

"Oh, sometimes we've got to move prisoners, one county to the next, when one that has charges in this county runs away and gets caught in another county or when they have charges in more than one county."

"Oh my! People who commit crimes all over the place."

"Exactly. I guess they never think of that when they're doing it, but it makes things more complicated for us later on down the line."

"I see that. So what kind of fellers are these? Really mean? Like murderers or something?"

"No, not usually," Ben continued as they walked along. "Most of them are more like guys you've known all your life. Some not as smart as others, most not smart enough to stay out of trouble. Others are sure they're smarter than everybody else. They're usually the worst ones."

She smiled as she watched a great blue heron open up its great wing span and fly away from the hatchery pools, balancing gracefully atop the cedar tree in the nearby field.

"Oh, the hatchery boys hate them," Ben commented, following her line of sight.

"Those beautiful birds?"

"Those beautiful birds can eat half a dozen yearling trout in two shakes of a lamb's tail and that don't

set well with them that just spent a year raisin'
'em," he chuckled.

"Oh, my. I had no idea," she said as she shaded her
eyes with her hand to look a little more closely at
the long-legged bird. "So you like being a deputy?"

"I do," he admitted. "It's always interesting, hardly
ever boring, or at least if it gets that way for a little
while, it doesn't last. There are some things we
seem to do over and over, like straightening out
fights between neighbors, even between husbands
and wives. Those are probably the worst, especially
when he's been beating on her and then she gets
mad if we haul him off, but..." he shrugged.
"Sometimes that's the way of it."

"So you do transports and break up fights. What
else?"

"Help people mostly," he answered. "Like folks
who come to our office because something of theirs
was stolen. Or people who get hurt because they
were in the wrong place at the wrong time."

"Like who?"

"Well, we took a young feller to the hospital last
week. He works down there at the railroad and a
bunch of those boys were rolling dice after work.
The sheriff has been keeping an eye on that and has
us breaking up those games whenever we can
because of the gambling. Anyway, this boy,
William Cooper, he just turned 19. He was only
watching but when two of those old boys got into an
argument over the money, one of them pulled a
pistol and started shooting. He accidently shot Bill

Cooper in the back of the neck. Now we got the one who did the shooting in jail for assault and Bill Cooper is at home, recuperating. Don't think he'll be standing around watching them boys shooting dice again anytime soon."

"I guess not," Jessica smiled. "It's not really funny, but...."

"Exactly," Ben smiled back. "A lot of our work is like that. Still, there's always something new or different coming down the pike and I like that part. I can't quite get that across to my mother though."

She nodded. "She doesn't like you being a deputy?"

He shook his head. "Not much. I imagine she thinks it's too dangerous for her baby boy."

"And is she right?"

"Well, it's not as safe as some things, that's true. But face it. I could go be a banker and get shot by a bank robber or work as what? A brick layer and have a load of bricks fall on me? I mean, everything is dangerous one way or another, isn't it?"

She laughed. "Well, I guess when you put it that way."

"Well, think about it. Weren't you in a bus wreck on your way here, to do what? Work in the CCC? Now, how dangerous is that? And yet, your bus collided with a hay wagon and you all were lucky nobody was hurt bad but it certainly could have been lots worse, right?"

She eyed him for a long moment before adding, "I

bet you just gave your mama fits growing up, arguing about stuff, didn't you?"

"Maybe. Sometimes. She would probably say so," he nodded, "but then look at you."

"Me? I'm not doing any kind of dangerous stuff."

"You don't think so?"

"Well, this is different."

"Is it? You're a rescuer, Jess Newman. It took me a little while to figure it out but that's you and that's part of what being a deputy is, too."

"What are you talking about?"

"You. Think about it. Why did you come here in the first place? Your family, right? They needed your help so you ended up here and then—"

She shook her head. "That doesn't mean anything. That's just taking care of what has to be done."

"Exactly," Ben continued, "but you'd be surprised how many people don't do that."

"Don't do what?" she asked in confusion.

"Just take care of what has to be done. To be perfectly honest, that's how a number of people end up in jail because they don't take care of the little things."

"If you say so," she answered dubiously while watching him closely.

"And then as fast as you get here, what do you do? You rescue Josef Schultz's horses."

"Well, of course. They were scared and hurt and…"

"And they needed rescuing," he grinned. "And then there was yesterday…"

"Well, now what else could I have done? Walked away and left Becky there by herself?"

"Some would have done that."

"That's crazy," she lashed back at him. "Who could go off and leave someone like that when the one thing she asked me was not to leave her alone? I mean, all I had to do was think if I were in her spot, how I would feel and—"

"Hey, I'm not accusing you of anything." He held up his hands in mock surrender. "I'm just laying out the facts as I see them," Ben added with a chuckle.

"Hmph," was her only comment. She dropped her eyes to her boots and watched her own steps for a few moments. When she looked up, it was to watch a lone fly fisherman, standing in the sparkling waters, the late afternoon's sun's rays glinting off his line, not far from where she and Percy Lee had spotted Ben and J.C. a few days earlier.

"I liked watching you and J.C. fishing the other afternoon. That was really something."

"It is something special, trout fishing. There's no doubt about that. Do you fish?"

"Yes, but not like that. Just for bass, rock bass, crappie, little perch."

"Rock bass. We call them goggle-eye around here. And little perch? Those are blue gill."

"Call 'em what you will. That's the kind of fishing we do on the Eleven Point."

"Me, too, and catfish, of course."

"Of course," she added with a smile. She waved her hand to disperse a sudden cloud of tiny insects that surrounded her face as they walked close to the water.

"Hatches," he commented by way of explanation. "Larvae hatches, like mayflies."

"Pfft!" She attempted to blow them away from her face with little success. "Pain in the neck is more like it."

"I guess I'm just used to 'em," he grinned. "I was twelve when Becky married J.C. He came here from up by Jefferson City and he was already a fly fisherman. He learned in Colorado on a trip out there with one of his brothers and then after they got married, he taught me."

"What a nice bonus for you, as the new little brother-in-law," she giggled.

"Yeah, it really was. Of course, J.C. showed up here the first time in a snazzy state senator's car so I thought he was pretty much the greatest from the first time we met—"

"Oh, he's the one! You said your sister married one of the state people who came to see about making this a park," she laughed again. "I didn't put that together before."

"Yeah, and now you know the whole story."

"Hmmm," she eyed him with obvious amusement. "I doubt that."

She bent down to retrieve something off the ground.

"Whatcha got?"

"Oh, a fairy stone."

"A fairy what?" He asked as he looked at the small stone in her hand with a hole through the center.

"A fairy stone. My papa used to find them for me when I was little. He said a stone like this had been touched by a fairy and that's why it had a hole clean through. He said they would bring good luck, the luck of the fairies. He'd put them on a string for me, to make a necklace or bracelet. Silly, I guess, but it made pretty fancy jewelry when I was a little girl."

He smiled as he cradled the little white stone in his hand. "I never heard of that before but it must have made you feel pretty special."

"It did." She finished with a smile that lit her face with the lovely memory and touched his heart unexpectedly.

A truck, loaded to the limit with building stone, lumbered past them on the graveled road. A couple of the CCC workers, riding atop the load, hollered and waved at Jessica as they went by. The squatting truck turned right at the spring and passed by the running blue water, turning again towards the construction site of the picnic shelter when a front tire exploded with a resounding boom. The truck lurched to a stop.

"Whoa!" Jessica jumped and then punched him in the arm. "Come on!" She challenged him and then ran towards the truck, arriving as did several of the workmen coming from the picnic shelter, including Captain Smith.

"Great Days of Glory!" Captain Smith clapped his hand to his forehead. "What next?!"

As if on cue, a dark cloud rolled across the sky, playing peek-a-boo with the sun. A stiff breeze bent over the wild flowers and tossed bits of leaves about their feet.

"Captain, I hate to say it…" The driver of the truck stood back to survey the damage.

"I know, I know, you're going to have to unload all of that stone to get a jack under this thing!" He heaved an exasperated sigh of disgust. "All right, men! Stop what you're doing and put your backs into it!"

Men scrambled forward and began to move the stones, handing them over, one to another. Without comment, Jessica stepped into the lineup and passed the heavy stones, right along with the others. Ben stepped back out of the way, standing beside Captain Smith. In short order, the flat bed was emptied and a couple of men pulled the tire out from under the bed of the truck before others jacked up the front end to remove the destroyed tire.

Jessica caught up to Captain Smith who was still chatting with Ben.

"Excuse me, sir," Jessica spoke up as the two

stopped speaking upon her approach. "I thought I would check and see what you found out about the horses and if you still wanted to use them to get that tree taken care of up at the Shine house."

"Yes, I think we've got that arranged." He looked up at the darkening sky and swift moving clouds. "As a matter of fact, if I don't miss my guess, the horses are up at your place or will be soon." The captain turned towards Ben. "I spoke on the phone to Josef Schultz earlier today and he told me he wasn't really up to driving his team at this point but he would trust them to the CCC man who rescued them a few weeks ago," he added with a grin. "And that would be you. He said he'd have his grandson deliver them back to the Darling place sometime today if you could get the job done tomorrow or the next day. And after this latest with another truck down…" He shook his head with a grimace. "I think that's a good decision."

"Yes, sir. I can take care of that. Tomorrow then."

"Tomorrow. I'll have a couple of the boys up there with a crosscut saw first thing in the morning."

"Maybe we'll just mosey on up to the house now and see if they're up there," Ben suggested.

"Sounds good," Captain Smith turned back towards the men on the downed truck. "Let's get that stone reloaded, boys!"

Fat rain drops began to fall amongst the leaves and then pelt down furiously.

"Come on! I'll race you!" Ben laughed as he started

towards his own house at a half-gallop.

"You? Race me? I'll beat you before you've even started, Deputy Ben Darling!" She shot up the trail past him, with a squeal and a giggle, as the rain poured down on them both.

A near breathless Ben Darling managed to tumble through his own front door barely ahead of Jessica Newman, both of them soaked to the skin.

"Holy smokes! You weren't kidding!" He was still laughing as he whirled about, catching her in his arms.

"Oh my!" she whispered and pulled up short, looking directly into his face. The two froze momentarily, taken aback at their own unanticipated reactions.

Then, Ben pulled her close and kissed her tenderly.

CHAPTER 9

As the sun rose the next morning, Deputy Ben Darling pulled out of Bennett Spring State Park headed west over gravel roads towards Dallas County. The county line zigzagged through the park. Deputy Darling's route would take him west, along that same line to a crossroads on Highway 32 where he and the Dallas County deputy met to transfer prisoners.

His mind drifted back to yesterday afternoon and a leisurely stroll along the spring branch. What he had said to Jessica was true. He did like being a deputy and for all the reasons he told her. Time didn't seem to drag as much in this job as in so many others. There was getting to be a fair amount of driving, which gave him time to think and he certainly needed a little of that now.

When he first met her, he had thought of her like everybody else, a smallish shy new government work force recruit who knew her way around horses. Now his thoughts were reeling in all sorts of new directions, none of which had a thing to do with the CCC. He loved the idea of seeing her dressed in something other than boys' clothes or old worn out army uniforms and he let his thoughts toy with that image for a few moments.

"How's tricks?" His Dallas County counterpart asked as he pulled up beside the waiting vehicle.

"Pretty much same old thing. Not much new." Ben replied. "Who've we got here today?"

"Eldon Walsh, some wise guy from up around St. Louis, as I hear it." The Dallas County deputy stepped a few feet away from the cars to sign the transfer papers and talk to Ben with the hope of not being overheard. "He's a suspect in a Rolla bank robbery but I guess he's been causing trouble in lots of places so he's got charges here, there and elsewhere. I don't really know. I just know my sheriff talked to your sheriff and they wanted him back this way so here we are."

"Yeah, here we are." Ben scribbled his signature across the bottom of the papers and walked back to the cars.

The Dallas County deputy opened his car door, helped the prisoner out and literally, handed him over to Ben Darling. Ben checked the man's hands, cuffed in front, and made certain all was secure before putting the prisoner into the back of his car. He waved to his Dallas County counterpart and headed back the way he had come. He was pleasantly surprised to recognize the face in the back seat as the one on the poster he and Cletus had looked over after the Rolla bank robbery. He hoped that would make Cletus feel better.

"You got a cigarette?" The prisoner asked as fast as they were rolling again.

"No, I don't."

"You don't smoke?"

"No, I don't," Ben repeated with a shrug. "Sorry."

"Cripes, it ain't bad enough I'm stuck in the sticks with the hicks and now, with a kid deputy that don't smoke." The prisoner shook his head. "Well, no matter. Won't last long."

"What won't?"

"Hanging around out here in the boonies, that's what. I shouldna ever left the city, that's for sure."

"Well, that may be," Ben added, as he downshifted to slow his car going down a hill on the loose gravel.

"I mean, what do you people do out here for fun? Ain't no picture shows, bars, dance halls, girlie shows. Nothing. Now I know why my old man left the farm and never went back."

"I dunno about that," Ben shook his head. "We've got movie theaters in Lebanon and Buffalo but we aren't much on that other stuff. Most of the people out here aren't looking for trouble, just trying to raise their families, take care of their kids, that sort of thing."

"Yeah, chumps. That's all."

"Call us what you will. Most don't spend a lot of time in jail either."

"Yeah, well, jail ain't so bad as long as you don't have to spend a lot of time there and I won't be there long."

"You don't think?"

"Hey, I know, buddy." A knowing little smile spread across his face that held no mirth. "It'll be taken care of."

"Well, we'll see." Ben let the conversation drop. He preferred the drive over where he could keep his mind on more pleasant diversions.

On a tight curve, he slowed and came to a complete stop at a fallen tree that blocked the road. His first reaction was one of alarm because that tree was not there less than an hour earlier when he had driven this same road in the opposite direction. He didn't get time to ponder the matter long as half a dozen men with flour sacks over their heads scrambled from the roadside woods. Two held shotguns trained on him and the others held clubs and the last one had a baseball bat.

"Outta the car, Deputy!"

Ben's blood ran cold at the sight of those sacks with eye holes burned in them.

"What'd I tell ya?" The voice from the back seat crowed with raucous delight.

Ben stepped out of the car, his hands held high and his prisoner, with hands still cuffed, stumbled out clumsily behind him.

"He's got the key on him." Eldon Walsh directed one of the club-wielding men who pulled the handcuff key from Ben's shirt pocket and quickly unlocked the prisoner's cuffs. The same man snatched the pistol from the holster on Ben's right hip.

"Told you, Deputy," the former prisoner chortled again. "Come on, boys. Give me one of those guns." He reached for the nearest scatter gun but the man holding it pulled it back out of reach.

"What're you gonna do?"

"What's got to be done. What did you think?" Eldon retorted.

"I think you need to clap them cuffs on this deputy and stuff him back in his own car. That's what I think. That's all we're doing here."

"Hey, you country boys think you know it all but that ain't the way it's done, if you want to walk away clean," Eldon Walsh began to protest. "Sometimes this business gets messy and—"

"All I can tell you is, this is what we said we'd do, nothing more. This ain't St. Louis or Chicago, you know. Now get back over there with the boys in the back and mind your manners. We go shooting a deputy, they'll be no survivin' for none of us. We may not be the smartest boys around but we ain't stupid."

"Yeah, well, that ain't what it's looking like about now. I'm telling you…"

"Now listen," Ben spoke up in his own defense. "You don't want to do this. First of all, there's way too many of you. You'd never be able to keep whatever you do here today a secret so you'd better think carefully before—"

Eldon turned to go where he had been directed but as he passed the other man with the shotgun he lunged for it.

"No!" The tallest man with a baseball bat hollered as he bashed Eldon on the right side of his head.

Ben's head snapped around at a voice he recognized.

The bat boy continued towards Ben and slapped him with an open hand. "And we don't need none of your lip either." He pushed Ben up against the car, turned him around and motioned to the one still holding the handcuffs to put them on the deputy.

The other men gathered around, tucking Ben's hands behind his back. While two were busy stuffing him onto the floor of the backseat of his own car, others were moving the tree out of the roadway. The bat boy had already climbed into the driver's seat by the time Ben's feet were bound and a blindfold tied securely over his eyes. He heard and felt his car start up but it only moved a couple of hundred feet, deeper into the woods, out of sight of the main road.

"Now you just stay here safe and sound for a little while, Deputy, and we'll be on our way," the driver chuckled.

"Why are you doing this?" Ben's brain was screaming but he remained silent.

He lay still as he heard them troop away from the car, guffawing and half-dragging their new companion with them. A few moments later, he heard another vehicle start up in the distance.

After a few deep breaths to steady his nerves, Ben began to wriggle and see how he might get loose but he quickly discovered it was not going to be easy. He tried rubbing the blindfold off first but with little success. With much struggling and wriggling, he managed to sit upright in the back seat but the effort had him sweating and puffing in the summer's heat and humidity. He had no idea how long he had been struggling but he had heard one or two vehicles go by in the distance on the main road. He thought about trying to call for help but since he wasn't sure how far he was from the road, he thought the effort would probably be a waste of energy at this point. He had to get rid of the blindfold to be able to do anything more. For just a moment or two, he leaned his head back and took a momentary rest.

It occurred to him that just a few hours ago, he was holding Jessica in his arms, enjoying a first kiss with her, a few sweet seconds that might have lasted longer if his father had not arrived at the back door moments after they did. Even so, the delightful memory and the thought of more such moments was enough to re-energize his struggles. A minute later, however, a new concern loomed.

Ben had not heard a vehicle stop but he was

suddenly aware of approaching footsteps. He held his breath, uncertain of what his next move should be. The car door clicked open and a hand reached in and undid the stubborn blindfold as Jake's voice echoed in his ears.

"Ben! Ben, are you all right? Geez, I'm sorry about slapping you earlier but..." He stopped talking as he reached in with both hands and pulled his younger brother out of the car onto the gravel. Jake removed the twine from his feet. "Where's that handcuff key?"

"I dunno. I think it went into the pocket of one of your so-called friends. I've got a spare in my right front pants pocket."

"Okay, I'll get you out of this. I'm real sorry, Ben."

"Jake. Jake." An unexpected lump came up in Ben's throat as he tried to speak to his big brother. His big brother who had been his idol until he had gone to jail for moonshining when Ben was still in school.

He tried again. "Jake, what are you doing with these guys? This can't be what you came back here for." He ended in almost a whisper.

"Ben, I swear. I had no idea. I went back up on Poker Ridge after I seen Junior Kendrix down on the river one day but he said they weren't doing nothing up there, nothing like this anyway. A couple of days after I got there, these boys, Eldon and Herbie, showed up from somewhere up north. I didn't know exactly who they were or what they were up to, but turns out Eldon is kin to Junior's family, a cousin somewhere down the line. They robbed the bank at Rolla and promised to share a little of it if'n Junior would hide 'em out for awhile. I never thought too much about it until Eldon went and got himself picked up over in Buffalo and they took his car 'cause it was stolen, too. Junior just said we were going to get him back. He told me on the drive over that he got the low down from somebody over there in Dallas County as to when they were moving him. But earlier today, when he said we were going to get his cousin, Eldon, I thought maybe he was bonding out and we were just going to give him a ride. You could have knocked me over when we pulled over this car and you got out! I had to smack you earlier to shut you up and get them boys moving before they thought any more about Eldon's idea of shooting you!"

"Yeah, well, I do appreciate that, brother. I suppose a slap is better than the business end of a shotgun any day. So now what?" Ben stood up, rubbing his wrists and flexing his stiffened shoulders.

"I told Junior I was done. I let him know I'd be slipping out, nice and quiet, the first chance I got and they wouldn't be seeing me no more. He said he understood and he didn't blame me none. He knew as soon as we stopped you. He's always saying, 'when it's kin, nothing else matters'. So, I'm gone from there." He pointed to his bedroll, the same one he had deposited on his mother's front porch a few weeks earlier.

"Here." Jake reached down into the center of the bed roll and pulled out Ben's pistol. "Junior sent this back to you. He told me to give it to you the next time I saw you. 'Course he didn't know that was going to be today, but no matter."

The deputy tucked the weapon back into its holster. "Thanks, Jake. I really do appreciate that."

"Well, I remember hearing you say something about you were paying the sheriff for it yet and Junior said he didn't need it around his place. When Eldon and Herbie showed up, Eldon had one that he used in the bank robbery but I guess it was in the car that they picked him up in Buffalo. He was pretty much a pain in the neck with it, messing with it all the time and it made Junior real nervous. Junior told me to take yours with me when I left so I did."

"So you going back to the folks' house?" Ben asked.

"No. That ain't a good idea. Besides, if'n Eldon and his pal Herbie decide to give Junior a bad time about me that'd be the first place they'd look. No, I thought I'd go up to Grampy Trundle's place for a bit. Junior might remember him but Eldon wouldn't know nothing about him and Junior wouldn't tell him. I know the folks are worried about Grampy now that he's all by himself. Maybe he could use somebody to look after him for a little while. I always liked that old man. It would give me a place to hide out and think things through maybe. I dunno." He shrugged. "It's about the best I can do for now. I just know I can't stay with Junior no more, not when it's got me in with a bunch that's contemplating killing cops, including my own baby brother. Junior said it was supposed to be Cletus Meyers doing the transporting for Laclede County.

I told him that wouldn't have been a lot better. Cletus was always real decent to me way back when."

"Well, I appreciate that, Jake." Ben pounded on his brother's back as he gave him a bear hug. "I really do!" he added with a belly laugh of relief. "It's been a rough day, brother. I'm glad you came back for me."

"Yeah. Me, too. I couldn't leave you like that. Sorry it took me as long as it did but I didn't figure you'd get too far and I didn't want to leave Junior and them too quick and give those other idiots too much to think about. Here." Jake held out his hand to his brother. "You had a rock in your pocket with the key. What's the rock for?"

"It's a fairy stone." Ben smiled at his brother's quizzical expression. Ben tucked the little stone back into his pants pocket. "I'll tell you about it someday, if it turns out to be important. Now I guess I've got to go explain things to the sheriff. This ain't going to be good, that's for sure. What do I say about you?"

"You can tell 'em the truth for all I care," Jake shrugged. "You don't have to tell 'em where I went next, do you? But if you tell Sheriff Sam your own brother came back and got you and didn't have no intention of being with a bunch that stopped one of his cars in the first place, maybe he'll understand. You can tell him I got away from them boys and I'm going somewhere to stay out of trouble."

Ben nodded. "Maybe I can. He's been good to hire

me and never hold your past against me before so…"

"Sorry, Ben." Jake heaved a sigh. "I know I haven't made life easier for none of you in the family."

"It's all right." Ben dropped his hand onto his brother's shoulder. "If this had to happen today, I'm glad you were here and especially that you came back for me. You want a ride over to Grampy's cabin?"

"No, I don't mind walking. It's not that far from here anyway, cutting through the backwoods. You going to be all right?"

"Yeah, I'm fine. I'm just thinking about what's coming next. I'm glad you're out of Junior's place. I'll tell Ma and Pa. They'll be glad, too."

Jake grinned and Ben caught a glimpse of the carefree big brother he'd known long ago. "I bet they will. Ma wasn't too pleased to see me that day down there in the park, was she?"

"No. The company you was keeping didn't set well with her."

"Tell them where I'm at and that I'll do right by Grampy. At least there, I can catch us some fish on a regular basis and maybe do a little hunting and trapping. I'll be seeing ya." He picked up his bedroll and walked off towards the woods, away from the road.

"Take care of yourself, Jake."

"I'll do it," he called back over his shoulder.

Jessica relished the extra sleep she was able to enjoy this morning since she didn't have to cook. She pulled the covers up over her head as the others got ready and tramped out of the barracks to the mess hall and their various jobs.

"Hey, Lazybones!" Percy Lee quipped, poking at her as he prepared to leave. "It's inspection day. Don't forget!"

"Hey, yourself!" She answered back without peeking out. "I'm taking the horses up the hill this morning. I don't have to get up so early for a change, but I won't forget about the inspection later. I'll leave my bunk straight. I always do."

"Yeah, you do. That's a fact. Lucky pup," he muttered as he trudged out the door with the others.

Hunkered down in her covers, she enjoyed not only the extra sleep but the time to remember and contemplate the day before.

The unexpected kiss with Ben had lasted only a few seconds before they heard his father at the back door.

"Hey, hey, I didn't know we had company," came his surprised comment at finding the two of them, soaked to the skin, standing in his living room.

They had broken their embrace, but little more, when he came in and she was afraid he would see her blush. "I came to check…on the horses," she stammered as she hurriedly pushed past him to run back out in the rain towards the barn. The team was there, just as the captain had said. She looked them over carefully, giving each animal a small measure of oats. She ran her hands over Frankie's front legs and was pleased to see there was no sign of the earlier injury.

Ben followed her a few minutes later. "Are you all right?" he asked as fast as he scurried into the barn, shaking the rain from his hair.

"Sure," she answered, more confidently than she felt. "Why?"

"Oh, just checking," he grinned. "You ran out of the house kinda quick there. Had my pa giving me a strange eye but I told him I'd catch up to him later."

"He doesn't know?"

"About you? No. I didn't tell him and I don't think Ma did either. Becky swore her to secrecy when she told her. Ma knows best how to handle these things. There ain't nobody better to have in your corner than my pa when it comes down to a fight but he ain't always the best at keeping a secret. He means well but he talks to an awful lot of people in a day. He'll probably be plenty mad when he does find out but that's trouble for another day, not today." He shrugged with a smile. "So how are your horses?"

"Josef's horses," she corrected him, "are just fine. Should be all ready for tomorrow without any problem. I guess I'll come get them in the morning and take them up to Becky's house." She turned back to the closest horse and patted his neck to ease the awkwardness she felt.

"By then, I'll be off picking up a prisoner." They stood in silence for a long minute. "Rain's letting up," he noted, looking towards the open barn door.

"Then I'd best be getting back."

"Back?"

"Back where I belong," she said as she glanced towards the door. "No need to give your pa any more to wonder about."

"Jessica." He reached for her hand. "I ain't worried about my father right now."

"Well, what I meant was..." she hesitated.

"I know," he whispered as he cupped her face with one hand and smoothed her damp curls back from her face. "It's all new. Just don't go too far away any time soon. Promise?" He kissed her forehead and turned her loose.

She felt the color rise in her cheeks as she turned towards the open door. "I won't," she managed to say before she walked back towards the spring.

She stopped there to catch her breath and try to figure out exactly what had happened and what had changed. She glanced down the way towards the gauge house and the still-under-construction picnic shelter but the men were all gone now, undoubtedly run off by the rain. She wandered in that direction, her eyes fastened on the water as she walked.

It was so beautiful here. The aquamarine waters sped swiftly by, with hardly a ripple at this point in their journey. She walked straight to the gauge house, a tiny yet tall cabin-like structure at the water's edge. Inside, she leaned out of one of the windows that overlooked the rushing water below. For a moment, she watched the trout slipping silently through the crystal waters. How peaceful it was here, she thought, unlike the tumult that currently held her soul captive. How could she suddenly feel so differently about Ben Darling? Just a couple of weeks ago, she'd watched him warily, trying to guess what he was thinking and if he intended to turn her into the authorities. Now, he had apparently changed his attitude completely. At first, she thought it was simply out of gratitude, for her staying with his sister in her time of need but after today, she could see it was more, much more. She wasn't sure how she really felt about him. And yet there was a rush of excitement when he did anything as simple as touch her hand or brush a curl back from her face. She tugged her cap down tighter over those same curls and climbed into the gauge house window where she could perch and watch the waters flow by.

The serenity of that smooth clear water seemed to calm her restless spirit. She cast her eyes about, taking in the exquisitely straight tall sycamores that lined the banks of the spring branch on both sides. Their magnificent green canopies seemed to offer even more safety from the dangers of the world. It occurred to her, after awhile, she had best not miss dinner at the mess hall and give the captain, or anyone else, anything more to ponder when it came to her behavior. Reluctantly, she climbed down from the window and started back towards the CCC encampment. She kept her eyes on the water but also on the ground in front on her feet, looking for another lucky fairy stone. She had lost track of the one she had found earlier in the day and she wanted another, to keep for luck and the memory of the day.

CHAPTER 10

At the back door of the mess hall that morning, Jessica slipped inside and made herself a quick sandwich from a large biscuit, some scrambled egg and bacon and a generous helping of jelly. "Now that looks real interesting. Breakfast for the traveling man, heh?" Spuds noted as he watched her work.

"Got to get going with the horses this morning," she explained as she started towards the back door with a wave. "Thanks, Spuds."

"No problem. Hey, you remember about the wedding, right?" he hollered, both hands already immersed in dishwater.

"Come again?"

"The wedding. In just another couple weeks now. Mary Beth and I are inviting all the CCC workers who want to come. Just want you to know you are more than welcome."

"Well, thanks Spud." Jessica was touched. "I appreciate that." She had deliberately avoided much of the socializing the other workers did together, claiming shyness and trying to keep a low profile, but she suspected it really hadn't helped much. Instead, she'd become known as the horse rescuer, as Ben called her. Even if she didn't go to the wedding, it was nice to be invited.

After a quick walk to the Darling place, devouring her breakfast on the way, Jessica found the horses already harnessed and ready. She was more than a little surprised at that but all she could think was that Ben had done it as a favor to her. She swung a leg up over Johnny with a firm grip on his mane and slid onto his back, just as she had that very first day. She loved the way these two responded so well to her every move and the three of them were soon traveling quite comfortably along the spring branch road, headed across the park on a sun-drenched morning. Although the constant rain was adding days and difficulties to the captain's work schedule, she couldn't help but notice the beauty on all sides. It lent an air of enchantment to the place that whispered of peace and tranquility, even the magic of the fairies, she thought with a smile, as she touched the new fairy stone she had tucked in her pocket on the walk home late yesterday afternoon.

Several of her co-workers waved or called a greeting as she passed their work stations, and even Captain Smith gave her a half-salute as she rode past the picnic shelter where he was once again supervising its ongoing construction.

She saw Percy Lee, engrossed in his efforts on the bridge as he and his team worked to cover the new concrete structure with freshly-cut sandstone. They had a long way to go, a lot of work to do, Percy Lee said every night back at the barracks. Still, he sure seemed to be enjoying what he was doing and she was happy for him in that.

The horses climbed the long hill on the way to Becky's house, turning into the drive at the crest of the hill. A pair of workers in CCC uniforms with their crosscut saw had already been at work and had the tree across the road partially cut into sections. Another slightly smaller tree lay beside it. It had been damaged by the first tree as it fell and they had determined that it too would pose a similar hazard in short order if not removed. "We looked at it and figured you could drag it off that a-way," Butch, the older one explained as she approached, still on horseback.

"That should be fine," she replied and slid off the back of the tall Percheron.

Jessica went to work, lining up the big black geldings and hooking them up to the first section of tree trunk the men had already cut free. They had lopped off a number of the bigger limbs and piled them out of the way on the far side, making her job easier. With a line in each hand and the excess thrown over her shoulder to keep it from dragging the ground, she walked behind the two horses, which made short work of the mighty job. Together, they soon had the trees out of harm's way, clearing J.C. Shine's driveway for the first time in many days. Before noon, the entire job was completed and the tree trunk sections pulled off into the nearby woods where they could be split for firewood or even cut for lumber at a later time.

"That ought to make Captain Smith happy," Butch commented good-naturedly as she returned, walking behind the horses, her hands full with their reins.

"I hope so," she answered. "At least we didn't have to tie up one of his precious trucks this morning doing this. He's really having a time, keeping up with it all, it seems."

"Sometimes, being on the low end of things as workers don't seem like the best place to be," Butch commented, "but other days, I look at the bosses and their headaches and I think maybe we're not so bad off." He laughed at his own philosophy. He picked up the long saw and followed his younger partner as they headed down the path back towards the park. "See you down below," he called out as they walked away.

"I'll just let Mrs. Shine know that we're finished and the drive is clear," Jessica called after them.

She led the horses over to an area of lush green grass in front of the house and uncoupled them where they immediately dropped their heads to the fresh growth they found at their feet. Jessica watched them momentarily and then turned away, confident they were not going anywhere anytime soon.

She knocked on the front door and called out. "It's just me. Jess."

"Jessica, for heaven's sakes. Come in." Hannah came to the door immediately. "How are you? I was wondering when we might see you again."

"Yes, ma'am." Jessica pulled off her cap and stepped inside. "I've been wanting to come back and see all of you again, especially those babies."

"Well, I imagine that's true enough." Hannah ushered her inside. "What can I get you? Something to drink or to eat?"

"I just wanted to let Becky know we got that tree out of her drive now and it's all off there to the far side in the woods. The wood will still be good for lumber or firewood later on, whenever they get around to making that decision but at least for now, it's out of their way."

"Well, bless you, Jessica and the CCC woodcutters for taking care of that. I know it'll be one less hassle for J.C. to contend with and he'll appreciate that. Zeb looked it over a few days ago and was trying to figure out when he would have time to do something about it. But you want to see the babies, don't you? Come on."

"Well, ma'am. If I could wash up a bit and wipe off the horse smell first that would be good."

"Of course. Go on. You know where the bathroom is."

After a quick clean up, Jessica was happily ensconced on the living room settee with a baby boy in her arms and a baby girl snuggled up next to her. Becky came in from the back room where she admitted with an embarrassed smile that she had been taking a nap.

"Oh, I'm so sorry for disturbing you," Jessica apologized.

"No, it's fine, really. I'm so glad you came. I wanted to talk to you and tell you something before you heard it from someone else." Becky's smile was broad.

"What are you talking about?" Jessica's brow drew into a worried frown.

"It's a good thing," Becky assured her as she sat down beside her daughter. "At least I hope you will think so. J.C. and I decided on names for the babies. Both of our families have a tradition of Biblical and family names so we're going to name her Elizabeth Fiona Shine, my mother's middle name and J.C.'s mother's first name, and then we'll call her Beth. Jeremiah is J.C.'s first name so we're going to name our son Jesse Jeremiah and call him Jess, after you. If that's all right with you?"

Jessica's eyes brimmed with tears as she kept them trained on the baby in her arms. "I never..." She attempted to speak but it came out a whisper. "I never imagined…"

"Sis! Becky!" Ben burst through the front door. "I need to use your telephone!"

"Benji, are you all right?" Becky stood up in alarm.

"Yeah, all things considered. How about you?" His eyes rested on Jessica with tears in her eyes. "What's up?"

"Nothing," she answered quickly, wiping the back of her hand across her face. "It's nothing really."

Becky reached over and squeezed her wrist.

"Ben, what's wrong?" His sister followed him to the kitchen where he snatched up the receiver and turned the crank on the wooden phone box on the wall.

"Lois," he called the local operator by name. "Get me the Sheriff, quick." He held up a finger for his sister. "Where's Ma?" he asked softly.

"Outside, I think. Hanging diapers on the line."

"Good. Hello, Sheriff. This is Ben. Sir, I'm sorry but I'm calling about that prisoner you sent me to pick up at the Dallas County line this morning. He got taken away from me a couple of hours ago by a bunch from over at Poker Ridge. Yes sir. They had a couple of shotguns. They dropped a tree across the road and when I stopped, they come running out of the woods. I sure am sorry." He listened for a moment. "Yes, sir. I'm fine. As fast as I could get to a phone, I called to let you know. Yes, I'll be there in just a little while to make a full report. Thank you. Yes sir. It's been quite a day. See you a little later."

"For heaven sakes, Ben. Thank the good Lord, you are all right!" Becky spoke as fast as he hung the receiver back on its hook on the side of the phone.

Jessica listened, eyes wide, as he told his story.

"Well, that ain't all of it, but I don't need Ma to hear it neither. The sheriff says he wants a full report when I get in there to the office but in the meantime I'm all right, mostly because Jake was there."

"Our brother, Jake? With the ones who waylaid you? What happened to your face?" She reached for his cheek.

"Yeah," Ben dropped his head with a smile. "That's how I got this. Jake slapped me."

"What?"

"It's kind of a long story but they was all wearing flour sacks over their heads. Jake told me afterwards he had no idea what they were up to this morning when they left, telling him they were going to get Junior's cousin, Eldon. He was the man I had in custody."

"Junior Kendrix! Why am I not surprised?!" Becky fumed.

"Well, once they had me out of the car, Jake come up and slapped me and told me to hush up. Then he convinced 'em to tie me up and leave me since Eldon was wanting to shoot me and leave me for dead."

"Oh my stars, Benji! You're right. Ma would have a conniption fit if she heard all this!" Becky sank back down on the settee beside Jessica and the sleeping babies.

"I'm not sure I don't feel the same way," Jessica half-whispered as she looked back at the peaceful infants.

"I know. I know and I'm sorry," Ben apologized, although he wasn't quite sure for what. "At any rate, they tied me up pretty snug and left me in the back of my car and then took off with Eldon." He grinned. "But not before Jake whacked him with the baseball bat he was carrying. I'm sure Jake gave Eldon one whale of a headache."

"Oh my!" Jessica's eyes grew wide again as he told his tale.

"Anyway, after they were gone quite awhile, Jake came back and untied me. He swore he didn't know anything about what they were doing until it was too late. He told Junior he was done with them up there on Poker Ridge. He had his bedroll and said he was going to go hide out at Grampy Trundle's cabin for a time. I told him Ma and Pa would probably be happy to hear that, anyway."

"Hear what?" Hannah came in through the back door as he finished speaking.

"Listen, I've got to go, Ma. I'm due back at work in town. Becky'll explain it all to you."

His sister coughed suddenly and he whirled to give her a quick hug. "Thanks, Sis. I owe you one."

"Oh, you have no idea!" She hissed in his ear. "You just wait!"

Jessica hugged Baby Jess close, working hard to suppress the smile that threatened to reveal more than she intended. Ben was incorrigible.

Jessica had waited days to hear her name at the daily mail call. She often saw Ben's father, Zeb Darling, come by and drop the CCC camp mail sack at the captain's office. These days he even waved and said hello to her but she had all but given up that he was ever going to bring her a letter. Today, he had even stopped to chat for a moment.

"I take it everything went well with the horses yesterday." He leaned out the window of his truck as he was pulling away from officers' barracks building.

"Yes, sir," she answered. "I took the horses back to your place afterwards, brushed 'em down and left them there for Mr. Schultz. Becky told me that she appreciated everyone's help getting that tree out of there."

"She sure did. J.C., too. In days past, I would have taken care of it right quick with my mules, Tick and Tock, but they got too old on me and I up and lost 'em both this winter. Just a couple months ago really, which is why I still got oats and bran up there at the barn. I got to say I miss them both and I just ain't quite got around to doing something with it yet. As it turned out, kinda glad I had it around the last couple of weeks. Guess you found 'em all harnessed up right yesterday morning?"

"Well, yes sir, I did," Jessica giggled. "I wasn't sure who did that."

"Oh, that was me," he admitted with a grin. "Just looking at that pair made me miss my mules. The horses are a lot bigger of course, but it was good to have my hands in the harness again, so I didn't figure you'd mind."

"No, sir, a little help, anywhere you can get it, is always welcome," she added.

"My pleasure, Jess. See you later." Zeb Darling waved as he drove away.

When Jessica's name was finally called today after lunch, she took her letter outside and found a quiet place along the mill race under the canopy of a sheltering sycamore tree to sit and read without interruption.

> *Dear Jess,*
>
> *Sorry it has taken me so long to write. Everyone here is fine. This leg has taken longer to heal than I expected but it is finally on the mend. The kids call your checks blue money and it has really helped. Had to tell Grammy the truth but she is fine with it now. Will have to hop a freight to get there. See you soon.*
>
> *Love, Your Brother*

The letter wasn't long but it told her everything she had been waiting to learn all these weeks. Everyone was well and her brother's leg was finally getting better. Grammy knew where she was and wasn't angry at her. Well, hopefully not anymore. She held the paper up to the light and then to her nose as she inhaled deeply to see if there was any aroma of home still on it. Without warning, she leaned forward and covered her face. A small sob escaped her but she rallied to squash the impulse quickly. She couldn't afford to have someone see her sitting here, bawling like a baby. Maybe more to the point, she feared if she gave in completely she might cry for a very long time. She wiped her eyes with the back of her hand and looked at the letter again before letting her eyes drift to the waters slipping silently by in front of her. A tiny hummingbird swooped low and winged swiftly to a nearby oak tree where he perched high in the branches and disappeared from sight. She heard approaching footsteps coming from behind.

"Jess. You finally got a letter. Was it a good one?" Percy Lee came around from the back side of the sycamore.

"Oh, yeah." She sat up straight. "It's from my brother and he said everybody at home is doing fine. I saw where you got several letters."

"My mom and my aunt and one of my sisters all wrote so it was good to hear from them. My mom lives in Caruthersville and my aunt is in Cape Girardeau. My sister got married last year and she and her husband are in the little town of Hayti so I got all the news from southeast Missouri."

"So now what?" Jessica asked wearily.

"Today? Oh, this is just dinner break, you know that. I got to go back to work here in awhile on the bridge. We're really starting to make some progress though. Have you seen?"

"I rode past there with the horses yesterday and from what I could see from the road, it was looking good."

"Well, you should come see it now. We're really starting to move. You know, we had to take all the stone off that we put up last week and start again. I guess somebody up the line doesn't like the way that double bathroom came out. They said the design wasn't good. It looks good to me but then I'm no expert. But then I think, who are most of the people who are going to come and use it and see it in the future? They ain't going to be stone or art experts. I bet most of them will think it looks pretty good, too." He shrugged and sighed. "Sometimes, I think these educated types worry about all the wrong things. What do you think?"

She laughed in spite of her fatigue, physical and mental. "Maybe you're right."

"Well, sure I am. Think about it. If'n folks are coming here to fish and camp, they ain't going to be worried about the design in the stones in the bathrooms or the bridge. At any rate, they made us tear all the stone off and start again. Now John Kelly, the main stone mason, he's got us doing it 'just so', but that's all right. It ain't like I'm in no hurry."

"What do you mean?" She turned part way around towards him with a frown.

"I mean, it's all fine and good to get news from family but it wasn't exactly what you call welcome news. Still, no jobs and no sign anything is getting better back home. Just more farms sold and folks leaving 'cause there's nothing left for them back there. That kind of thing." He sighed. "It sounds like I'm going to need to stay here awhile so I don't have to be in no hurry with that bridge or anything else. I just need to sit back and settle in and do what I can here."

"Hmm." Jessica turned back towards her own letter.

"So what about you?"

"Come again?"

"What did your letter say? What are your plans?"

"Oh, well, I don't know." She deliberately re-folded her letter and tucked it back into its envelope. "The folks from home, they don't say much. Just that they are all good, kids are growing, Grammy's fine. There's no work, of course, but that's nothing new."

"And you? What are you going to do?"

She let her gaze wander back to the moving blue-green water. "I can just do one day at a time, Percy Lee. I can't make myself think no further ahead than that right now or it'll make me go crazy. I know it will!" She drew her knees up tight to her chest and dropped her folded arms over them.

"That's fine! That's just fine!" Percy Lee laughed and slapped her on the back. "We'll be right here together, working side by side. You know, I never had a brother before. Just four older sisters and now I do. I got you and you got me! Brothers, working and a-bunkin' side by side."

Jessica hid her face in between her elbows. "Oh, Percy Lee," she let out a half-moan that ended in a low laugh. "You have no idea."

"Sure, I do!" he continued to chortle. "You and me against the world. We'll stay here and keep workin'. At a dollar a day, after a month, they give us five dollars at pay day and they send the rest home, now that's something."

"Yes, we have that, something to send home and a little in our own pockets." She dropped her knees and climbed to her feet. "I'm on mortar duty again today but tomorrow it's back to the kitchen. Spuds is leaving. Did you know?"

"Yeah, I heard something about a wedding. He's getting married and staying here at Bennett Spring, right?"

"Yes, the wedding is a week from Saturday. Spuds said we're all invited. Did you know that?"

"I heard. Speaking of such, I'm going with a bunch down to the river, what they call the confluence, where the river meets the spring, after work. They've been going down there to do some fishing and swimming after work. Wanna go with us?"

A demure smile crept across her face as she shook her head. "No," came her soft answer.

"No? Why not? Didn't you tell me you love to swim and you did all the time at home on the river?"

"Yeah, it's true, but…"

"But?"

"But what? This ain't home is all. It's different here. I can't really explain it."

"It's all right. You don't have to." Percy Lee's good humor was not easily deterred. "It's just so hot and humid by that time of day, I thought you'd want to go, too."

She tried to cover her discomfort. "It's no big thing really. I just need to study more on that school stuff they've been dumping on us. The mortar hauling is flat hard work and getting up early again to do kitchen work has me falling asleep before suppertime, so I better spend my spare time studying instead of swimming."

She stretched her arms upwards, bent over and stood up straight again. "Right now, it is time to go back to work." She pointed towards the line of other workers who were traipsing off towards their various work sites.

"Yeah, you're right. Back to being a bridge slave. Never knew nothing about stone work before I came here but John Kelly has been real patient to teach me so I'm starting to feel like I actually know something about being a real stone mason."

She smiled in earnest this time. "Well, that's good, Percy Lee. It'd be nice to come out of this knowing how to do something new."

"That's the truth." He nodded as he walked off towards the triple-arched bridge. "See you later at the barracks."

Jessica watched him walk away before she started towards the Bennett Spring Church of God. She thought about Percy Lee and the others and their swimming plans this afternoon with more than a touch of envy. That's all she needed was to be messing around the water and fall or get pushed in. She had managed to keep her gender under wraps, despite some suspicious looks and the complications with Ben and Becky and their family. Sometimes, like now, it still made her feel so guilty, like she was flat out lying to Percy Lee, Captain Smith and the others and they had been so kind to her. Now at least, with Jesse's letter in her pocket, she knew this odyssey would soon be over.

CHAPTER 11

Four o'clock in the morning had never been his favorite time of day and today was no different. Ben waited impatiently outside his place of employment as deputies from Dallas, Laclede and Camden counties gathered on the front porch of the Laclede County Jail on the corner of Adams and Third Street in Lebanon. Two deputies pulled up to the front of the building in a Phelps County sheriff's car. They had driven into town late the afternoon before and stayed the night at Miz Josie's boarding house. Sheriff Sam's telegram, telling them their bank robbery suspects may be hiding out in western Laclede County, had brought them all the way from Rolla.

"Boys!" Sheriff Sam Allen brought all the small talk to a halt as he addressed the group. "We're about ready to roll out. First, I want you all to step outside here now and check all your weapons one last time, long guns and pistols both. We're likely to need 'em all. So far, this bunch has robbed at least three banks that we know of and kidnapped one of my deputies. Up to this point they haven't shot nobody yet, but I ain't willing to wait until they do. And I'm afraid that's exactly what'll be next if we dawdle around with these fellers much longer. So I want to be clear from the get-go. We're going out there with the plan to clean 'em out of there. Whatever it takes. I'd prefer to bring 'em all back and lock 'em up and I don't want no deputies hurt in all this but if they don't want to come along easy and peaceable, then we'll take 'em however it has to be done. One last weapons check and we're ready to go."

He stepped outside and went around to the back of the building where he climbed into the passenger side of his waiting car. Ben Darling waved to Cletus Meyers who was staying behind to keep the office open and slipped into the driver's seat of the sheriff's car. Ben drove around to the front of the building and five other lawmen's vehicles quickly lined up behind him as he drove towards Bennett Spring.

"Best time of the day," the sheriff commented as they drove along.

"You think?" was all Ben could say.

"Best time of the day for catching mischief-makers. The night owls have finally gone home to bed and the few who do still work a regular job aren't up yet. Best time to catch 'em all still in the sack."

"Well, I never thought of it that way," Ben admitted

with a sheepish grin.

Sheriff Sam didn't have much more to say on the long drive and Ben tried to keep his mind on the business at hand. Even so, he found his thoughts drifting back to the unexpected joy of discovering Jessica in his sister's living room when he stumbled in there the day before yesterday. Thinking about it now, Ben regretted that he was so caught up in his own trials and tribulations of the moment. Still, it was a wonderful surprise to find her there, looking so content with his niece and nephew in her lap. How was it he had not seen from the very first day that she was a lovely young lady, hiding out in men's clothing? How did she manage each day not to be discovered? Now, he couldn't look at her any other way. It did explain why she was always looking down, always pulling that silly cap down low over her eyes. Those beautiful blue-green eyes, almost the same color as the spring waters. He did see tears though the other day and he had never found out exactly what that was about. He would have to remember to ask Becky later. If he begged her hard enough, she would tell him. Then he remembered Becky would be looking to make him pay for the last minute explanation to Ma he had dumped on his sister as he dashed out the door. An unexpected smile crept across his face at the memory.

"Don't know what's on your mind this morning, son," Sheriff Sam interrupted his musings "but I wouldn't be smiling like that when we pull up to Poker Ridge here in a few more minutes."

"Oh-uh, yes sir. No sir. Just something that I was remembering from the other day with my ma, that's all."

"Uh-huh, well, I don't remember ever looking like that as a younger man when thinking about my mother, that's for sure."

Ben's face colored unexpectedly. "No, sir, it was actually my sister. It was her house I got to first the other day when I called you and my ma was out back hanging clothes. She came in asking what was going on and I left my sister to explain it all. My ma hasn't exactly been happy about me working as a deputy is all."

"Most women aren't. That's a fact," the sheriff added.

"Yes sir. So I kinda left my sister to sort it all out with her and I was just thinking when next I see her, she, Becky that is, will be looking to pay me back for that one."

Now even Sheriff Sam let a half a smile crack his face. "Yes, I expect she will."

Jessica bit back a groan as she rolled out of her bunk that morning. When Captain Smith first told her he was going to be switching her from job to job, she thought that sounded more interesting than working the same job, day in and day out, but these days she wasn't so sure. Jumping back and forth from a day shift of hard labor to the earlier shift of cooking breakfast was exhausting. She tried to move around quietly in the dark as the others continued to snore.

Their barracks smelled worse every day. Too many unwashed bodies crammed into too small a space. The constant dampness of too many days of rain and not enough sunshine and fair breezes, the usual June fare for this part of the country, did not help.

Outside, on the barracks porch, she hesitated for a moment. The low rumble of approaching vehicles on the gravel was not a particularly unusual sound in the middle of the day but it was enough to make her stop at this early hour. The lights of half a dozen vehicles, following each other in close formation, came swiftly around the curve and continued past the turnoff to the barracks, without ever slowing. Each vehicle bore a sheriff's star and was filled with men with guns. In the dawn's light, she couldn't recognize faces but she knew Ben had to be among them and she knew, too, where they were going and why. Her first thought was to run, not walk, to Becky's house but then she thought better of it. Why not let her continue in bliss and ignorance for as long as possible? Her next impulse was to pray, and that she did as she lowered her head and closed her eyes tightly. Please protect them, Lord.

She walked on towards the wash house, once they were out of sight.

The kitchen was already less cheerful with Spuds Emerson gone or maybe it was just her imagination. The new officer in charge seemed nervous and lacked Spuds' easy style that made her feel like the place was run by a good friend rather than a typical supervisor. She concentrated on making her biscuits and staying out of sight.

Jessica said another quick prayer especially for Ben this time as she rolled dough and punched out 'hockey pucks' as Spuds called them. She wondered how Spuds was doing, what he was doing and how he would like married life here at Bennett Spring. She thought back to her conversation with Percy Lee yesterday and all his talk of the future. What did her future hold?

As soon as Jesse arrived, it would be back to Riverton for her. How in heaven's name did Jesse intend to make that change over anyway? He had never gotten around to explaining that little part of this scheme. She decided she would worry about that bridge when it was time to cross it and besides, by then Jesse would be here. That means it would be his problem, not hers.

She would be happy to see Gabe and Grace and Grammy when she arrived home and even Jesse when he got here, but there would be so many from Bennett Spring that she would miss. Percy Lee was goofy but he had been a good friend and she had never had a girlfriend like Becky before. She was older but a true friend despite their age difference and someone, it seemed, who understood her better than most of the people who had known her all her life.

And then there was Ben. She wasn't sure what to think about him except that every time she saw him, he made her smile or laugh even when he wasn't trying to do so. Like the other day, when he ran out on them when Hannah came in the back door. She had never seen anyone dance a conversational two-step better than Becky did when telling her mother Ben had to get back to the sheriff's office on an urgent matter but that he was fine and just stopped by to use the phone. Even when he was not there, just the thought of him made her smile and warmed her heart.

Maybe Spuds was the lucky one, she decided. He was getting married in another week and he knew just what he was going to do, where he was going to be and maybe most important, who he was going to be with. The rest of them weren't so lucky. And what would life be like once she was back in Riverton after all the excitement and activity she had experienced over the last several weeks?

Essentially, she had been complaining to Grammy that morning before Lyle showed up at their door about being bored with her life. While she missed the home folks, the thought of returning to that life was now nearly unbearable. What was worse, however, was the thought of never seeing Becky or Percy Lee again. No, she slowly let the thought unfold as she started to knead the last batch of biscuit dough, the worst would never be seeing Ben Darling smile at her again.

Sheriff Sam Allen directed Ben to roll up, slow and quiet, within view of the old frame house that squatted in the tall unkempt grasses of Poker Ridge. Never a prosperous outfit, the old Kendrix homestead suffered from too many years of moonshining, petty crime and general neglect. The other cars followed closely behind Ben but the surprise element the sheriff had hoped for was quickly lost in the cacophony coming from a makeshift pen behind the house, where Junior kept his coon dogs. The sheriff quickly dispersed the men to surround the house, despite the sounding canine alarm as the first rays of the rising sun peaked over the horizon.

"Junior Kendrix!" The big bass voice bellowed over the coon hounds and echoed down the hollow to the river below. "Junior Kendrix, this is Sheriff Sam Allen! You boys come on out peaceable now and we'll have no problems."

There was a rustling in the house as a face appeared at the back window and a voice still husky with sleep replied. "Sheriff? Sheriff Sam Allen? Is that you?"

"It is, Junior. You boys come on out now and there'll be no trouble."

"Sheriff, we ain't done nothing. What are you doing out here so early bothering law-abiding folks?"

"Never you mind the excuses, Junior," the sheriff answered. "We'll sort out the particulars later. All you need to know right now is we got warrants for the lot of you."

"Warrants?" The voice from the house cracked with indignation. "What warrants? We ain't done nothing."

"Junior, I ain't gonna stand out here all morning trading words with you. You boys need to get the move on….NOW!" And with that the sheriff fired a single shot across the front porch, shattering a brown jug that was perched on the railing.

"Have mercy on me, Sheriff!" Junior squealed, tumbling backwards out of the window. He scrambled towards the front of the house. "We're a-coming!"

Junior was the first out the door, with his hands halfway over his head, and was followed by several others in various stages of undress, including one fellow who was completely without clothing. The next to the last man out of the house carried a pair of overalls which he tossed to his naked companion, who dropped down to sit in the dirt and struggle into the too small overalls. As the last man straggled out the door, Ben noticed with keen disappointment that Eldon was not amongst the haggard-looking, unshaven bunch.

Following the sheriff's lead, the circle of lawmen moved in closer, their guns at the ready. Sheriff Sam waved his free hand, the one not holding his pistol, still drawn and trained in an all-business manner on the group, towards Ben. He and another deputy began moving about, checking the grounds.

"So Junior, what's been going on out here? Is this all of you?" The sheriff continued the earlier conversation as if they were sitting in an office and not standing in the dawn's early light in Junior Kendrix' front yard, with the morning breeze whipping the weeds at their feet.

"I dunno, Sheriff. Not much. Did you just come out here to make small talk at this hour? You coulda called me on the phone for that. I got one now, you know. A real phone that connects all the way to town."

"Well, that's real nice, Junior, but no, I got a few other things on my mind right now. Where's that feller named Eldon Walsh?"

"Who?" Junior's head jerked up like he had been kicked. "What do you mean?" He nervously glanced back along the line of his partners in crime as he spoke.

"What do I mean? I mean, where is Eldon Walsh? You go deaf or something?"

"Well," Junior stalled and his eyes roamed past the lawmen like he was trying to recall something forgotten. "He ain't here, Sheriff."

"I can see that, Junior." The sheriff's patience was wearing thin. "I asked you where he was."

"Uh, he went back up north. Where he come from, is all."

"Where he comes from. And where might that be?"

"Uh, uh, I don't rightly know. Somewheres up the other side of the far north counties."

"You don't rightly know, my Aunt Georgie's knickers! Junior I've had about enough of—"

"Sheriff, you better see this!" Ben called out from a small outbuilding directly behind the house. A working still and a full wooden-stave barrel full of its latest brew were tucked in behind a wooden wall that cut the interior in half and was fronted by half-barrels that looked as if they could hold feed or grain or the like. Instead, they held nothing at all and were mere camouflage for the illegal operation.

"Not doing nothing, heh, Junior?" The sheriff repeated as he strolled back towards Junior who, along with his companions, was now sitting on the ground. "Where's Herbie Potts?"

"Herbie who?" Junior continued to echo like an owl but the sudden twitch of the dark-haired man who had earlier come out of the house with no clothes was enough for the sheriff.

"Herbie?" The sheriff turned towards him. "Deputy Reuben Smith," the sheriff barked towards the line of lawmen. "You got that sketch with you?"

"Yes sir." The thin and energetic Phelps County deputy stepped forward and pulled a folded wanted poster from his back pocket. "Right here."

Sheriff Sam Allen only needed a moment to compare the drawing with the man seated before him in the bulging overalls.

"Herbie?" The sheriff tried again. "Where's your buddy Eldon?"

Herbie shrugged as if disinterested. "I dunno. Ain't seen him in a couple of days."

"Is that so? And how is it he went back up north without you?"

He shrugged again. "Don't know, Sheriff. He just

did."

"He just did, heh? Well, we'll see about that."

Sheriff Sam Allen motioned for two more deputies to go inside the house and begin a search. "Look it over good boys," the sheriff commented as they trudged inside. "Our Mr. Eldon Walsh may not be as far away as we think."

The two deputies spent several minutes in the small house while Ben and his counterpart dumped the barrel's contents and began to dismantle the still.

"Moonshining is still illegal, Junior," the sheriff reminded the leader of the bunch seated on the ground. "Prohibition or no prohibition."

"Well, Sheriff, a feller's got to have a little fun every now and then. I guess we'll have to go pay for it for awhile but that's all right," he added with an evil grin.

Sheriff Sam Allen turned his attention from Junior for the moment and took a few paces away from the house to meet Ben who was coming back up the hill as others took over in finishing up with the still.

"I'd like to wipe that smart-alecky smile right off of his face by coming up with that bank robber and his take from that robbery, right here and now," the sheriff muttered. "I don't suppose you can identify any of these ones as being along on the day they took Eldon away from you," the sheriff asked Ben without expectation.

Ben looked over the lot of men before him and was simply thankful Jake was no longer among them.

"No sir, I'm sorry. I can't. They all wore sacks over their heads that day and to be honest, when Eldon started talking about shooting me, I wasn't paying too much more attention to what they looked like but more—"

"Sheriff!" One of the deputies stepped out of the house, both hands filled with what looked like dirty white rags.

"Dang!" The word popped out of Junior's mouth almost before he realized it.

"Well, now that's a nice little extra, ain't it, boys? Deputy Darling, do you happen to recognize these?"

The sheriff took three white flours sacks from the deputy's hand, each with two burned holes in the bag at just the right measure for a pair of eyes.

"Yes, sir," Ben grinned broadly. "These do look way too familiar."

"Well, I'm glad to hear that," the sheriff chuckled.

The other deputy stepped outside. "That's it, Sheriff. No sign of Eldon or anybody else in there. You think he figured out we was comin'?"

"Oh, it's possible." The sheriff rubbed his chin as he pondered the situation. "I don't think he'd have heard anything, but he might have figured that after he and this bunch waylaid a deputy that we weren't going to just sit around and let that pass. Still, it's a shame. Well, we got Herbie. That's enough to connect the rest of the bunch as accessories to the bank robbery for hiding him out. It ain't a lot but it's a start.

"Let's load 'em up, boys," the sheriff hollered and the deputies proceeded to get their prisoners to their feet, get them handcuffed and figure out which cars to use to haul them back.

"What's the matter, Ben?" the sheriff asked as he watched Ben continuing to stare at the house, deep in thought.

"I was just wondering is all..." Ben did not finish the thought as he walked slowly around the house, squatting down and looking over the crumbling foundation.

He slipped up the stairs and quietly walked back inside where he stopped and listened for several seconds before proceeding. Inside of the pantry off the kitchen, he carefully moved his hands across the wooden walls covered in worn tongue-in-groove panels. Once part of a kitchen, not unlike his mother's that had held home-canned goods, this one was now cluttered with scraps of lumber, leather, wire, oily rags, old tools and other junk men tend to collect.

At the back of the pantry was what appeared to be a full length bench built into the wall, but when he began to push and pull at the seat portion, the lid lifted revealing a storage space that opened right down into a tiny crawl space beneath the house. Ben looked in but in the dark he couldn't see much, only that it led down into the small cramped space below.

He stepped back and retrieved what looked to have once been a broom handle. Leaning it against the wall, he kicked it in the middle, snapping it into two pieces. Then he collected up several of the oily red rags, tied them onto the sticks and dampened them with water from a bucket standing by the outside door. He sprinkled both rags with a small amount of kerosene in a rusted container he found sitting in the corner of the floor of the pantry. A lit match from the cook stove and both rag torches began to leach thick black smoke. Ben fired them down the space beneath the bench and clamped the lid back down.

Back outside, he circled back around the house to where the sheriff and the others were now watching with unspoken curiosity as smoke began to seep out of cracks and fissures in the foundation. One tiny cramped window space with a board shoved in at the back of the house also had smoke leaking around it. All remained silent for a few seconds more before a faint coughing sound could be heard coming from beneath the house.

"Eldon!" Ben stepped over to the makeshift window and pried the wooden cover loose. "You might as well come on out of there! We know you're in there and if you don't come out pretty quick, we might just burn the whole house down over the top of you, if we have to."

"What'd you say? Burn my house!" Junior squealed from where he stood beside a Camden County deputy's car. "Eldon, you get your sorry backside out of my house this minute, you hear me? You been nothing but trouble since the day you showed up and now they're talking about burning down my house on account of you! Get out, you hear me?!"

For a long moment, it looked as if nothing more was going to happen and then a curse and more coughing could be heard, close to the crawl space window.

"Some hideout your place turned out to be, cousin!" Eldon wriggled, snorting and spitting, head first as he came out the window, his nose and eyes running from the smoke.

"Suit yourself," Junior responded. "You're certainly welcome to go hide somewheres else the next time you're running from the law!"

"That's it, boys!" the sheriff called out over the two spatting cousins. "We've got 'em on harboring bank robbers, moonshining and kidnapping a law officer. That should keep 'em all locked up for awhile. Let's get back to town!"

"What about my dogs?" Junior's attention suddenly shifted.

"What about 'em?" the sheriff replied. "Ain't got no dog complaints in this case."

"Who's gonna feed 'em and take care of 'em?"

"Well, now Junior, I'd say once we get you booked in at the jail, you better make a phone call or two to figure that out," the sheriff declared, as he continued towards his own car.

Two other deputies pulled Eldon Walsh to his feet and clapped a pair of handcuffs on him.

"Behind his back!" the sheriff instructed as he stopped once more. "Put him in the back of your vehicle, Charlie, face down on the back seat."

"Face down?" A quizzical expression knitted the deputy's brow as he looked back at the sheriff to make certain he understood correctly.

"Yep, face down and you can tie his feet together too, if you find something to tie 'em with. He should be glad I don't have you stuff him down on the floor as well. That's the way he left my deputy out here tied up in his car, wasn't it?" He turned to Ben, who looked down in embarrassment.

"Well, yes sir, it was but—"

"No buts about it," the sheriff concluded. "Fair's fair and that sounds fair to me."

The sheriff whacked Ben on the back. "Nice work by the way, going in there and smoking him out. What made you think of that?"

Ben let out a horse snort sigh with a relieved chuckle. "When I was a kid, we used to visit a friend of my mother's on the other side of the valley. She had an old house with all kinds of little closets and crawl through spaces. My mother said the house had been done up that way decades before when it was owned by a family of Quakers before the Civil War. They used it to help escaped slaves along the Underground Railroad. Of course, us kids thought it was great to hide in one closet and come out in another room or slip into the pantry and drop down into the crawl space under the house. Just couldn't help but wonder if this house didn't have some similar little traits."

"Well, good thinking," the sheriff added.

Ben walked past Eldon and his two escorts as they proceeded to stuff him into the back of their car.

"I shoulda shot you when I had the chance," Eldon growled as they pushed him in.

Sheriff Sam leaned over as he followed Ben to their car and growled right back. "You better be glad you didn't or this day could have ended a whole lot different than it did. This here is a down-right-happy-ever-after-ending as far as you boys are concerned!"

The sheriff climbed into the passenger side of his vehicle. "Let's go, Ben."

CHAPTER 12

It was the last wheelbarrow of mortar for the day and Jessica was thankful for it as she set it down. She stood before the first of six diminutive cabins that lined the hillside, overlooking the long meadow west of the church building. The mixers were situated in the middle of the row of cabins and she and another man hauled the filled wheelbarrows to the individual sites. She stretched her back and looked across the land as it rolled away to the spring branch, the same view the folks who would one day rent these cabins would enjoy from their front windows.

The stone mason for the first cabin came down to where she stood to scoop out the mortar as he prepared to lay the last row of stone for the day along the base of the new cabin. She rolled her shoulders forward to ease their stiffness and continued to look towards the water. A dark layer of clouds rolled overhead, threatening another round of rain.

She wandered towards the busy worker and watched as he expertly scooped a precise portion of mortar with his trowel, using no measuring device except his own eyes. He smoothed a fresh layer of it across the flat stones he had laid previously in the afternoon and began to drop the next layer of stones on top. He tapped each one into place with the handle of his trowel, leveling each with obvious precision.

A familiar black car with gold stars on its front doors rolled up and parked along the roadside, opposite her wheelbarrow.

"Well, hello," Ben Darling greeted her as he stepped out of the car.

"Hello, yourself," she answered as she walked towards his car from the cabin. "What are you doing out here today?"

"It's Thursday," he smiled.

"Well, I guess it is," she admitted. "Can't say as I pay a lot of attention to the days except for the ones we don't have to work."

"I appreciate that. I don't miss Thursdays generally. Ma wouldn't like it if'n I did."

She giggled. "I imagine that's true."

He yawned and stretched.

"You tired or just bored?" she asked with a half-pout of a smile.

"Oh no, just up awful early yesterday and still

trying to catch up."

"Oh!" Her blue-green eyes snapped at his words. "I saw you all yesterday!"

"You did? When?"

"When six or seven sheriffs' cars rolled through here with the rising sun," she said. "I didn't see your face specific but I figured you were going after the bunch that took away your prisoner a couple of days ago. Was I right?"

"Right as rain, ma'am—"

"Shh!" she shushed him quickly. "Careful what you say, Deputy!"

"Oh, Jess!" His face colored as he apologized and clapped his hand over his mouth. "I'm sorry. I just didn't think—"

"It's all right," she whispered with a giggle at his chagrin.

"Jess," the stone worker called her name as he walked down from the cabin. "I'm done for the day. You taking the wheelbarrow back?"

"Yeah, Carl, I'll get it." She turned serious as she whirled to face him. "The stone work looks real nice along there. I'll get that wheelbarrow back where it belongs. No problem."

"Well, it's good to be done for the day." Carl stretched as he spoke. "I've got my tools." He held up a lumpy gunny sack. "I'll take 'em down over by the spring branch and wash 'em up. See you back at the mess hall later. I'm going back that way before the rain starts coming down again." He squinted at the darkening sky.

"Good point," she agreed without moving. "See you later."

She and Ben watched him walk back past the church. "You just never know who is around." She rolled her eyes in Ben's direction as soon as her co-worker was out of earshot. Fat raindrops began to fall down around them.

"Come on!" He tugged at her sleeve and scurried towards the empty cabin in front of them and she quickly followed.

The door did not have a latch yet so it swung open easily at his touch.

"Aren't these divine little cabins?" Jessica exclaimed as fast as they were inside. "They are just so sweet, with the way they are set up with a living room, little bedrooms, even a kitchenette, as they call it, in some of them." She walked over and ran her hand over the top of the new steam radiator tucked under the window on the side of the main room. The shiny new green asphalt floor tiles seemed to reflect the outdoor greenery and the large front window opened up on the idyllic scene of the tree-lined stream below.

"Yes, they are, what did you call them, sweet? Yes, sweet it is." He pulled her close, wrapping his arms around her. Her face turned up naturally towards him and he kissed her. Her response was immediate and she didn't pull away as she had the first day in his parents' house.

"Oh, Ben." She dropped her face and leaned her head against his chest. He hugged her so tightly he was afraid he might hurt her but she didn't complain as her arms encircled him and hugged him back.

"Are you all right?" he asked after a few seconds of silence.

"Oh yes," she breathed a whispered answer. "I'm very all right."

"Good. Me, too."

They stood wrapped in each other's arms, neither in a hurry to break the embrace. If there was music, she thought, they could have danced the afternoon and evening away right there. Together, they watched the rain through the large front window, looking over the idyllic scene of the trees in the meadow, as the land sloped away towards the spring branch. Ben was thankful there was no light in the cabin so that no one from the outside could catch a glimpse of the two of them inside.

Finally, Ben broke the magic. "I hate to say it, but I've got to go to my mother's house. You want to come to dinner?"

"Oh, you know I'd love to, but…"

"But what?"

"I just don't want to make any trouble, here at the camp or at your house."

"And what kind of trouble would that be?"

"You know." She dropped her arms and turned

away from him. "It's just like a few minutes ago, one of us slips and says the wrong thing or looks the wrong way and then..." She couldn't believe she was the one speaking because the whole time, her heart was screaming go, go, go. Jesse is on his way and once he's here, you'll be gone and then you'll be sorry you didn't spend every minute you could with Ben and the Darling family.

"Hmmm." Ben rubbed his chin as if he were in deep thought. "What if I promise to be sober as a judge and not come anywhere near you the whole time? I can be good and I know you can! You've managed to keep this whole camp in the dark about who you really are for weeks now so I know you can manage it for dinner tonight. But it's up to you. If you really don't want to come..."

"Oh, you brat! You know what I want!"

"Well, then." He opened his arms wide and she flew to him. He gave her a last passionate kiss and reluctantly turned her loose and followed her out of the cabin door into the rain as they ran to his car.

"So then Sheriff Sam fires a shot across the front porch and busts a jug that's sitting there. Now that gets Junior's attention right quick," Ben chortled as he related the story at the dinner table of the deputies' exploits at the Kendrix house the day before.

Becky and J.C. sat on one side of the table, their little ones tucked snuggly into Zeb's favorite overstuffed chair nearby. Esther, Hannah, Zeb and

Jessica rounded out the rest of the group, listening intently to Ben's account. "And then when we're all back at the office later, the sheriff said he didn't even know that jug was there! He just meant to fire a warning shot across the porch to wake 'em up!"

Zeb was laughing so hard, Ben paused to let his father catch his breath.

"Oh my heavens!" Zeb gasped as he wiped his eyes. "I bet that did have ol' Junior a-hoppin'!"

"Oh yeah, pretty much," Ben added. "He hopped right out the front door with the rest of 'em right behind him and one of 'em naked as a newborn baby."

"Benji!" his mother interjected.

"Sorry, Ma. Sorry, Esther," he chuckled. "But he was!"

"Good grief." His mother shook her head and bent over her dinner bowl of beans and smoked ham hocks.

Ben's story continued to unfold with the day's events. Zeb began to chuckle again when he described Eldon's smoky exit from the crawl space.

"So you remembered Miz Lucille's house over there in Plad?" Hannah's interest in his story was renewed.

"Yes, I did," Ben answered his mother. "I always remember how us kids were just fascinated with them closets and little crawl through spaces."

"Well, I don't imagine the ones at Junior's house

were developed for such a noble purpose as the Quakers and the Underground Railroad a-helping escaped slaves," Hannah sniffed.

"I'd say that be true." Zeb wiped his eyes again and took another bite of cornbread.

"Jess, I apologize again for the plain country fare tonight." Hannah turned to their guest. "Didn't know we were having company so it's just plain country cooked ham and beans and cornbread."

"Oh, it's fine, Mrs. Darling. It's real fine. It reminds me of my grammy's cooking at home." She smiled and stole a sideways glance at Ben, who kept a sober face despite the gleam in his eye.

"So you got 'em all to the jail with no more troubles?" Zeb asked, taking them back to Ben's account. "You know there's quite the story going around the county at the moment, of how this bunch kidnapped one of Sheriff Sam's deputies a few days ago and—"

Becky reached across the table and in doing so, tipped over Esther's half glass of milk. "Oh, gosh, Ma." She jumped up as if she had been kicked. "I'm so sorry. Sorry, Esther. Here, let's mop that up and then I'll get you some more milk. What a mess! I swear since I've had these babies I get more clumsy every day!"

"Becky, Becky." Her mother handed her a dish towel. "It's all right really. You're just tired, honey. I warned you of that. One baby is more than enough to tire a new mother near to death, I cannot imagine two at once!"

"Oh, I'm fine, really," Becky continued to prattle as she gave Ben a knowing look. He leaned over to whisper in his father's ear. "If you wouldn't mind for Esther to come over for the weekend while she's out of school, that would be a great help."

"Well, of course. Esther?" Hannah turned towards her youngest daughter as she dropped the milk-soaked towel into the wash basin. "You don't mind, do you?"

"No, Ma. I'll go help with the babies any time, you know that. I'll get my chores done here and then…"

"We'll work it out, Esther. I'll help you with your chores and then I'll be up to Becky's, too."

Becky set a fresh glass of milk beside Esther's bowl of beans and exchanged glances once more with Ben as she sat back down.

"We got everybody back to the jail and locked up. Those Phelps County boys took Eldon and his partner back with them so that's two less we got to deal with. Still, it's got our jail pretty full so that's keeping Cletus busy, looking after them all."

"I bet it does." Becky giggled.

"Becky, don't be hateful," her mother admonished.

"I don't mean nothing by it, Ma. Honest."

"'Course we'll be taking Marvin Sparks to the Nevada asylum any day now," Ben went on, "so that will help with the prisoner overcrowding. Just waiting on the judge's orders and for them to tell us they got an open bed."

"Marvin Sparks." Zeb shook his head. "There's another one that will like as not, never get straightened out."

"He's had a hard life, there's no doubt," Hannah commented. "He is truly one of the 'least of these' as Jesus called him and his kindred souls," she added, not unkindly.

"Least amount of sense, anyway." Zeb stuffed the last of his cornbread into his mouth.

"Zeb, don't be disrespectful," Hannah scolded. "If Jesus could take pity on the ones with demons in them…"

"Well, I don't claim to be nearly as good as all that," Zeb mumbled. "And the likes of Marvin Sparks ain't exactly good at keeping his demons to hisself, if you know what I mean."

"Oh, he ain't too bad," Ben chuckled. "At least, he's not a screamer or a crier, like some of the drunks."

"Benji," his mother cautioned him again, casting a sideways glance at Esther. "Enough shop talk from the sheriff's department for tonight."

"That's probably a good idea," Ben agreed. "J.C., how's the father business going? You learning all about, how was it you put it that day—diapers and Pablum?"

J.C., who had remained remarkably quiet during the earlier discussion, seemed to come back to life. "Sorry. I do believe this is the longest I've sat still in days and I'm afraid I was about to doze off. Lack of sleep and all." He grinned his apologies. "I talked to my mother long distance last week and now that the babies are here, I think she is finally going to move."

"Really?" Hannah remarked. "That's wonderful news."

"Yes, it is," Becky added. "J.C.'s been after her to come on down here ever since his grandmother died last fall but she's been all worried about the farm and all."

J.C. shook his head with a smile. "The animals have all been sold but she kept hoping she would be able to sell the farm as well. I told her nothing is selling now so just close up the place and we'll get her moved and worry about the rest later. I think I've found her a little house not too far from here that she can rent, at least for the time being."

Hannah patted Becky's hand. "Oh, I do hope Fiona will be happy here. She is such a delightful person and now, more help than ever with the babies, right?"

"Oh, yes." Becky continued. "She's like you, Ma. She's all about the family. Her sister lives here and now with these newest grandbabies, it will be wonderful to have her here, too. Of course, she has her other grandchildren up there close, J.C.'s older brothers' kids by the Holt's Summit farm, but I know she is all excited about this pair from the letters she's written to us. It will be good for all of us."

"So your mother is moving from Jefferson City to

here?" Jessica asked softly.

"Yes," J.C. nodded. "She's lived for years with my father's parents on their farm but they're both gone now and I know my brothers have been keeping an eye on her but still, it's time she got off that farm. She doesn't need to be taking care of all that. Getting her down here, close to us where she can be near her youngest grandchildren, is a much better idea."

"And you are happy that your mother-in-law is going to live close by?" Jessica asked Becky directly and then looked down in embarrassment as she realized how the question must have sounded, but Becky took no offense.

"Oh, yes. She is a sweetheart. She's so funny. She's originally from New York with a little bit of Irish accent yet and it's even just fun to listen when she talks. The first time I met her, she threatened to throw J.C. out of the car and keep me!"

The whole family laughed and Jessica looked immediately at J.C.

"It's true!" He held up his hand as if taking an oath. "She did!"

"You know J.C. told me once the heart of this valley, the heart of Bennett Spring really, are the people who live here." Becky smiled and reached over to pat Jessica lightly on the back. "If that's true, Fiona Shine will fit in here just fine."

"You really are all about your family, aren't you?" Jessica observed solemnly as she looked around the table.

"Oh, I suppose we are," Zeb sighed with a straight face. "Just the way of it although if you ask me, this is just a way for J.C. here to get out of so much baby care and nappie-changing. He gets his mother to move down here and then he don't have to do so much of it."

J.C. sat up straight in mock indignation. "Now that's certainly not true. Becky says I don't have to worry about feeding the babies right now." He flashed his charming smile in her direction. "She's taking care of that part, even with the two, but now diapers, that's another question. I'll have you know I'm becoming quite proficient at not sticking myself with those diaper pins. And getting that diaper on straight. Now that's important because heaven knows, if you don't, it's pretty much worthless."

Zeb stared at him, open-mouthed. "You really are a-changin' those things?"

J.C. looked directly at him. "I am, sir. Why?"

"Well, I don't know as I really ever heard a man tell it, if'n he did," Zeb answered with a sly grin.

"Just never you mind," Becky admonished her father. "Don't you be telling him any different, thank you very much. He can't help with the feeding right now but he can sure help with the other end of things!"

A low rumbling laugh escaped Zeb. "Well, it's a new generation, I guess" was all he said as he shook his head.

"Yes, it is," Hannah agreed. "And they got their own way of doing things which is just fine. Now, I've got fresh strawberries and whipped cream. Who wants some?"

CHAPTER 13

A couple of hours later, Jessica lay on her bunk, listening to the rain continue its incessant drumming on the roof of the barracks. Despite the noise, she had a smile on her face as she drifted off to sleep. Dreams of Ben Darling's arms encircling her, the steady rhythm of the rain on the roof, the lingering taste of sweet strawberries.

Jessica's eyes flew open and she sat up so fast she nearly cracked her forehead on the bunk overhead. She could feel it. Something was wrong. Something was terribly out of balance this morning in the worst way but she couldn't name it. Outside, on the front steps of the barracks, she could hear it. A strange and ominous roar engulfed the entire valley. She was still standing there in the light rain when Sgt. Patrick O'Hara hurried past her and burst in the front door.

"On your feet, boys!" he bellowed. "No sleeping in this morning. All crews are needed at the hatchery as fast as you can get your boots on! It's flooding, boys, and it ain't a pretty sight."

Jessica didn't wait for the rest. She hurried towards the source of the mighty roar and was amazed to see the beautiful serene blue-green waters of the spring branch churned into an angry chocolate-colored torrent. Yes, it had been raining for days, but she had never expected anything like this. At home, she had seen the Eleven Point flood many times, like any other river, but not like this. The sudden volume of it was awesome and more than a little terrifying as if at any moment it might burst forth from its already crumbling banks and flood the entire valley.

"Wow! Will you look at that?" Percy Lee arrived at her side, still buttoning his uniform shirt. "That's really something, ain't it?"

"Yeah, it's something," Jessica agreed. "Not sure what they want us to do about it though."

"Over here, men," the sergeant beckoned.

They lined up with all the others and got their instructions as rakes and long-handled brushes were handed out.

"Look," the hatchery manager began to explain at the sergeant's direction, "at times, there's too much water and other times, not enough. If that head gate up the line gets stopped up with debris, then the fish, especially the ones down below, don't get enough air, enough oxygen and they'll suffocate right there in the water. It also puts a lot of stress on them and then they just up and die on us. If too much water comes shooting through, it crushes them. If the water rises too high, then it will flood all the pools and mix all the sizes together. We might not be able to prevent that but if it happens, we'll have to watch close because it is easy to end up with way too many fish in one place and that's another mess." He stopped speaking long enough to wipe his brow against the inside of his elbow. "We appreciate your help, boys. Anything you can do will put us that much ahead and believe me, we're going to need everything we can get to save these fish."

Back and forth, they walked along the length of the hatchery pools, doing what they were told, stopping every few steps to clean screens and scrub away the collected debris. It didn't take long for their steps to turn to a trudging pace, one stop to the next, and the wooden implements they carried slowly turned into lead in their hands.

"Did you get some coffee?" one of the others asked Jessica as they passed, anonymous damp figures working and walking in the rainy dawn as they continued around the pools. "They've got coffee and some rolls up by the hatchery building. Better get up there and get you some. It ain't like the breakfast we usually get, but sure is better than nothing which is what we got so far this morning."

Jessica nodded and kept going in the direction he indicated. That could help explain the headache she felt at the base of her neck. Lots of work and no breakfast didn't help. She saw Percy Lee, leaning on his broom in front of the table holding the coffee and rolls.

"Hey, Jess," he greeted her with his mouth full.

"Hey, yourself." She returned and eagerly gulped a cup of the strong coffee.

"Geez, Newman, what are you doing still wearing a jacket this morning?" The worker beside her at the table looked over as if she had taken leave of her senses. "It's hot enough to cook rice out here in this damp and you're still wearing a shirt and a jacket both. I'm ready to strip off and work more naked than not, no matter what the captain says."

"Keep your shirt on, Barton." Captain Smith came up behind them as she reached for a second roll. "Kid, you and Jackson get up there and check that head gate again. The hatchery manager showed him earlier how to clean it and watch the water flow, right?" He raised his head in Percy Lee's direction and Percy Lee nodded eagerly.

"Yes, sir. He did. I can show Jess here what to do."

"Good, then get to it!" the captain barked and the two grabbed their long-poled tools and scampered upstream, walking along the slippery muddied bank.

"Lookie there!" Percy Lee stopped and pointed at half a dozen railroad ties that were tossing and turning in the churning waters like toothpicks rather than timbers that weighed hundreds of pounds. Jessica remembered seeing stacks of ties up along the stream bank, near the construction of the picnic shelter by the spring. They slammed into one another as they bumped and bashed along in the formerly beautiful serene stream now turned violent.

"Them waters are just plumb full of meanness this morning!" Percy Lee exclaimed as he continued to lead the way, edging perilously along the concrete sidings of the head gate. He stopped to poke at the accumulated leaves, twigs and other natural flotsam that had once again gathered against the manmade barrier.

"Right here," he instructed while shoving the long-handled broom in his hand down along the front of the head gate. "Like this." His hands slid down along the handle but as he gripped it to pull upwards once again, the lower part caught suddenly and jerked him off balance.

"Percy Lee!" Jessica screamed above the roar of the water coming down from the spring but it was too late.

Her friend tumbled into the drink, his boots making a splash as they flipped over his head. He came up suddenly, his eyes wild and panicked as he thrashed helplessly against the extraordinarily strong current.

She ripped off her jacket and jerked wildly at the laces on her boots as she pulled them off and dove full length into the water. As she knew it would, the icy water hit her like a punch in the chest, instantly snatching her breath away. She swam with the current, keeping an eye on Percy Lee's floundering figure. She raced forward. She had to reach him before they went over the dam. She was close enough to hear him coughing and sputtering even over the thundering frigid water. He disappeared beneath the surface but she kept her eyes trained on the place where she expected him to resurface.

Percy Lee popped up a short distance in front of her. He flopped and whirled, still fighting the foaming flood waters and with another couple of strong strokes, she was close enough to reach for his shirt collar. Her fingers were already stiff with the cold but with one more kick, she made a huge lunge and grabbed his shirt collar and pulled back. If she could just make it to shore, her thoughts kaleidoscoped one into another. It was then that she caught a glimpse of the fast-approaching dam.

Jessica stroked furiously in a sideways motion but it was an effort in futility. She saw Percy Lee's boots flip first. Her cramped fingers closed even more tightly on his shirt collar. She allowed the rest of her body to go limp as they went over the waterfall together. The icy waters closed overhead and she tumbled, head over heels, kicking and struggling as her lungs burned, screaming for air. She broke the surface in a frozen daze, gasping for breath. She still had hold of Percy's shirt collar but he was as much out of the shirt as he was in it. She twisted around to get a better grip and saw his ashen face, with eyes closed. His dead weight pulled against her and her heart shuddered.

She heard her own scream end in a sputter as the torrent pulled them both under again. When the churning water spewed them up one more time, they were even further downstream. For the first time, she caught a glimpse of the others, slipping along the banks. Even over the thundering waters, she heard them yelling and calling as they ran helplessly along the spring branch. She saw a long handle extend out across the water, here or there, but it was a short reach in desperation. She and Percy Lee sped past, continuing on their watery journey of disaster, seemingly destined to end in tragedy.

The beautiful triple-arched bridge was fast-approaching. If she couldn't get to shore before they passed under the bridge, they might be all the way downstream to Miz Suzie's washing hole before they got stopped. Percy Lee would never last that long. He might already be gone. She couldn't be sure but that thought was enough to spur her on to one last desperate effort to reach the shore.

Suddenly, she felt hands, the strong hands of other CCC workers who stood knee-deep in the frothy swirling flood waters as they pulled her and Percy Lee to safety, just before they would have swept beneath the bridge.

Jessica collapsed momentarily on the graveled bank beside Percy Lee. They laid him on his back but there was no movement of any kind on his part. Jessica struggled to rise and immediately fell upon him.

"Percy Lee!" she croaked, her voice breaking as she tried again. "Percy Lee!" She pushed herself up to her knees and shook him by his shoulders. "Wake up! Don't you dare die! Do you hear me?"

There was no response and she rolled him over on

his back and beat on him mercilessly. She rolled him back and pushed on his stomach. Water spewed from his mouth. She pushed him onto his side and continued to push and beat.

"Jess. Jess, it's done. He's gone. Let him be now." Captain Smith was wet to his knees, one of those who had waded in to help pull them out of the deadly waters.

"No! No, he can't be dead. He can't be!" She pulled away from the captain's grip and continued to push and pull at her comatose companion. "Percy Lee!" Her desperation had now turned to sobs. "Don't you do it! Don't you leave us!"

A black car with a gold star came across the new bridge, wending its way around the last remaining barriers. It stopped on the road and the two occupants scrambled towards the crowd of men surrounding Jessica and Percy Lee.

"Jess!" the captain barked at her.

Percy Lee's corpse suddenly coughed and convulsed and he began to wretch up even more water.

"Quick, boys! Get him upright!" the captain commanded.

Jessica climbed slowly to her feet. Her one remaining shirt, sopped and dripping, clung tightly to her thin frame as did her wet trousers. The others stepped back, in shock and surprise, as the truth could no longer be denied.

"Jess!" Her head snapped up at the familiar voice.

"Jesse!" She cried out when her brother ran forward to embrace her.

Ben Darling was by his side as they reached the uneasy knot of men, who were torn between celebrating the return of one of their own from the dead and the unexpected revelation of a stranger in their midst.

Her head was spinning. The cold that had claimed her totally was now causing her body to react like any other chilled entity in the warm humid air. She was covered in condensation which caused her to shiver uncontrollably. She turned back to see Percy Lee on his feet, standing unsteadily beside Captain Smith, who was now staring at her. Jesse released her and she felt incredibly light-headed as if she was floating once again in the water.

Ben was beside her, asking, "Jess, are you all right? Jess, can you hear me?"

She turned to face him, but her eyes could not find him. No matter how hard she looked, the light was gone and she could see nothing but darkness. Her head swam as she swooned but she could feel strong arms around her and familiar voices echoed in the distance.

"Captain Smith, I'm taking her to my sister's home up on the hill. I'll keep you posted, sir but for now, I'd say Jess Newman isn't doing very well."

"I'd say you're right, Deputy. We'll get Percy Lee over to the infirmary for awhile. I'd appreciate it if you'll check in with me later."

"I'll do it, sir." Deputy Ben Darling carried the still comatose girl back to the car with a swift stride, accompanied by Jesse Newman, who trotted along at his side.

The afternoon sun's rays slanting through the Venetian blinds danced across her face, bringing her back to the world that waited. The overwhelming fatigue that had engulfed her earlier was gone but it still took a few seconds to recognize the room and the single bed in which she had been sleeping. Twin cribs on the opposite wall told her what she needed to know. She looked down at the heavy flannel night gown she was wearing and she was simply thankful for its soft, cozy warmth. She spied a robe draped over the end of the bed.

Voices in the kitchen guided her as she made her way down the hall to find her brother, Ben and Becky, all visiting, laughing and holding Becky's twins.

"There she is." Ben Darling sat at Becky's kitchen table and raised a glass of tea in her direction. "How are you doing?"

"Much better," she added, feeling suddenly more than a little bit self-conscious. "What's...what's..." She hesitated, not even sure what she wanted to ask.

"What's going to happen next?" Ben put her concerns into words.

"Yeah. I guess that is the question."

"Well, we were just discussing that but I'm not sure

we have an answer."

"This isn't exactly what I had in mind, Sis, as far as a nice quiet little change over," Jesse spoke up from where he stood, leaning against the kitchen counter, holding a sound-sleeping baby Jess.

"Sorry," Jessica added with a shrug and a sheepish grin. "Can't say I thought of that when I was jumping in after Percy Lee. I just couldn't stand by and let him…How is he? Do you know?"

"Yes, he's fine," Ben replied. "I went back down there just a little while ago. They checked him out at the infirmary but they let him go back to his bunk in the barracks. They said he needed to rest today and he should be fine by tomorrow."

"Oh, good." Jessica visibly relaxed at the news.

"Yeah, good for him," Ben agreed, "but not so good for you."

"What do you mean?"

"Here, have a seat, Jessica." Becky stood up and handed off her daughter to her brother. "Would you like something to drink? Or eat? I made some fresh raspberry turnovers this morning before things got so exciting. Or I could make you a sandwich."

"Hmm. Raspberries and tea sound good." She smiled at her hostess. "And thanks for the nice sleep. I do feel better." She turned her attention back to the deputy. "What do you mean, not so good for me?"

"For either of you, maybe. Captain Smith is not too

happy down there, trying to sort out what kind of deal you two were trying to pull off and wondering if he should be calling the sheriff, his superiors or who."

"Oh, my heavenly days! Now what?" Jessica dropped her head in her hands, her elbows resting on the table. "What did he say? Did you tell him why we did it?"

"Not my place to do that." Ben chuckled and held up his hands in surrender.

"Well, what's your best advice at this point?" Jesse cut straight to the heart of the question.

"I suggested he wait until he talk to the two of you," he said, obviously enjoying the moment as he leaned back in his chair, cradling the sleeping infant. "I told him I thought I could make sure you were both down there in his office tomorrow morning and maybe you could get it sorted out then."

"You think?" Jessica looked up tentatively.

"I think that's all either of you can do." He smiled at her. "He's in a pickle too, you know. I don't think he's anxious to tell his higher ups that he's had a gal hiding out, undetected, in his company for what, six weeks? Makes him look pretty foolish but it's hard to tell exactly what he might do. I'd say you go see him in the morning. Be honest and see where it takes you. It's really all you can do."

"I suppose that's true." Jessica leaned back with a heavy sigh. "Well, then I want to think about something else. Something good. Give me that little baby boy. Jesse, did you know? His name is Jess, too. They named their baby boy after us. Oh, Jesse, tell me all the news from home. How did you get here? How's Grammy and Gabe and Grace?"

"Here." Her twin brother stepped forward and handed her the sleeping bundle he had been cradling. "They're all fine, just fine. Worried about you, of course.

"Getting up here was quite the trip because I didn't have no train ticket since I gave mine to you. Of course, we all knew how and where to hop the afternoon freight train coming out of West Plains but we also always jumped back off at Hopson's Corners a few miles down the line. This time I caught the midnight freight and just kept riding west. Had to watch out for the railroad detectives 'cause they're always looking to throw people off, but made it without any real trouble until I got to Lebanon." He stopped speaking and looked sideways at Ben who picked up the narrative.

"We got a call from the railroad yard that they'd caught three guys on a freight train and they wanted a deputy over there and the sheriff sent me. One of them actually ran off and got away from the railroad detectives before I got there and the other one, we did have a warrant on him for theft out of Stoutland so I hauled him and this feller here over to the jail."

His smile grew wider as he continued. "And then when I asked his name and he told me Jess Newman…well, I told the sheriff after they found no warrants on him that I knew he had family out this way that had been looking for him. Since it was a pretty slow day, I asked if he didn't mind I'd just give him a ride." He stopped to take a sip of tea while still balancing his niece on the other arm.

"Then, of course, we get out here and we discover you rescuing somebody and in all kinds of mischief! Imagine that!"

"Oh stop!" Jessica tossed the burp rag she had on her arm at him. "I wasn't—"

"Wasn't what? Rescuing Percy Lee? What else do you call it? There's a dozen CCC workers down there who would say different, if they was asked."

"Well, that certainly wasn't my purpose, to make more trouble. I just couldn't let poor Percy Lee drown right there in front of me." She looked down as Baby Jess squirmed and yawned.

"Lucky for him, you were always the swimming champ of Riverton," Jesse added with a laugh.

"I suppose so," she sighed.

"So tonight, Jessica, you can stay here with us, and Jesse you are welcome, too if you don't mind sleeping on the couch." Becky began to make plans. "Ben, I'm sending you over to Ma and Pa's for the night but before that, let's think about dinner. We can…"

Jessica looked around at each of them and was suddenly very thankful to have found such a warm welcome amongst new friends. Come what may tomorrow, she and Jesse were blessed to be well fed and have a safe place to stay tonight.

Deputy Ben Darling escorted Jesse and Jessica Newman into Captain Wilbur Smith's office the next morning. Both were dressed in civilian attire and Jessica particularly did her best to keep her eyes downcast, looking neither to the left or right, as they climbed the natural rise to the officers' barracks building, just to the northwest of the hatchery.

Captain Smith was seated behind his desk, which was covered, as usual, with various government forms. As fast as the three of them filed in, Captain Smith signaled for Ben to close the door, which he did.

"So there really are two of you? Two Jess Newmans?" Captain Smith spoke first as he looked from one to the other of the two siblings who stood before him. Ben Darling leaned back against the door, determined to stay out of the conflict he could see coming.

"Yes, sir." Jessica nodded. "This is my brother, Jesse Newman, who actually enrolled in the CCC several months ago, at West Plains."

"I see." The captain nodded. "And where, pray tell, have you been the last couple of months?"

"Back home in Riverton, sir. A little town down the way from West Plains, where we're from. With a broken leg. I was in a wagon accident the week before I was supposed to come and well, I didn't want to lose my place so this was our plan. Did you know during the Civil War, a lot of men drafted into the army sent a surrogate, a substitute, someone to

229

take their place so they didn't have to go to war? That's all this was, really, a sort of surrogate. Just for a few weeks until I could get back on my feet and get here myself."

"Look, this is a very interesting history lesson, Jesse, but it doesn't apply in this situation. You should have told somebody somewhere along the line and then the decision would have been made—"

"Yes, sir. A decision that could have left our family out in the cold. I don't mean no disrespect, Captain," Jesse interrupted, "but like most of the ones here, we're here because we need this job and the money that goes with it. We didn't tell anyone and we didn't ask no one's permission because we couldn't afford to."

"Well, that may be but in the meantime, I'm not sure what to do with the two of you. I'm sure there's been some kind of law broken here. Deputy, what would you call it? Theft? Fraud?"

"I don't pretend to know, really." Ben stood up straight from where he had been leaning against the back of the door. "I mean, if it's fraud, it means you didn't get what you were promised in some sort of business deal."

"That's right." Jesse leaned forward with a glint of excitement in his eyes. "You didn't get cheated, did you? Didn't you get a good worker for the money the government has been paying? Hasn't she earned her keep and then some? Didn't I hear she tended to the horses in the hay wagon bus wreck that happened the first day she came here? And didn't that help to keep the peace between you and the other CCC workers and the locals? And what about yesterday? Didn't she save one of your very own? Doesn't exactly sound like she's been shirking her responsibilities around here, Captain. Now I'm here to take her place, take my proper place really, but to be honest, I don't know that I can do as good of a job as she has, but I'm sure a-gonna do my best to make sure you're not disappointed with the Newman family name and—"

"Newman!"

"Yes, sir?" came the double answer.

"Do you always talk this much? One of the things I have to commend your sister on is that she's a lot more of a worker than she is a talker!"

"Well, sir." Jesse dropped his eyes to his feet but he couldn't completely hide the partial smile that appeared. "I do tend to talk too much when I get nervous or excited. It's just well, I can appreciate your position, too, sir. I mean, wouldn't the best for all be for me to simply take my proper place as Jess Newman, CCC recruit? We're not looking for any trouble, sir. I can assure you. If there's something else you need us to do to make things right, we'll be happy to—"

"Shut up." The captain rested his forehead on the palm of his hand. "Just shut up, Newman. Get your backside over to the barracks and clear out her gear and put yours in there. We'll try this and we'll say as little as possible. I can't imagine how this is going to work." He shook his head. "Jess, Jessica, is it?"

"Yes, sir," she answered.

"Do you have a place to stay? A way to get back home?"

"I, uh, well…" She glanced sideways at Ben.

"Yes, Captain. That's being taken care of." Ben stepped away from the door.

"Well, that's at least one problem avoided. Go on. Get out of here, both of you."

The twins bobbed their heads and quickly left his office.

"Thanks, Captain." Ben hesitated a moment longer. "I really don't think they were trying to do anything more than what they said."

"I take it you've known about this for some time?" He raised an eyebrow in Ben's direction.

"Honestly, not as long as you think." Ben peeked through the window, watching the other two standing in the driveway. "After the birth of the babies, then it all became clear," he fudged his explanation. "Thanks again. I appreciate you not being hard on them, all things considered."

"How can you be hard on a pair like that? He's right. She's already rescued us a couple of times and then…" The captain leaned back in his chair. "Well, now that you mention it, it does put a whole different light on that business with your sister and her babies, doesn't it? Jessica indeed. I tell you, even if this story makes it on up the line, who's going to believe it?!"

CHAPTER 14

Jessica slept more soundly than she had since leaving home nearly two months ago. For the second night in a row, she slept in the single bed in Becky's twins' nursery. She had hardly noticed as Becky came and went during feeding times in the middle of the night. Jesse was gone, having taken his rightful place in the barracks. She had barely had time to introduce him to Percy Lee, after their talk with Captain Smith. Percy Lee had stared at her the entire time she was in the barracks as if she had suddenly grown two heads. The others stood at a distance, looking and gaping, trying, she knew, to come to some kind of resolution with the facts. A woman had been hiding out in their quarters for weeks and they had not known. She felt bad for having deceived them, but there was nothing more to be done about it now. She showed Jesse where to put his things, hurriedly collected her own, stuffed them into her rucksack and cleared out as quickly as she could.

She stretched briefly this morning and thought how good it felt to not have to pretend anymore but now there were new worries, like how she was going to get home to Riverton. More importantly, was she ready to go?

It didn't make any sense really but there it was, just the same, a feeling, an intuition that said it wasn't quite time to go home yet. She tried to shake off such a ridiculous notion as she got out of bed to cradle a whimpering little one.

"Good morning, Jessica," Becky chirped as she came in to pick up the other baby. "How are you doing this morning?"

"All right, I guess. Becky, how do you do it? I would think you would be exhausted with two babies a couple of weeks old but every time I see you, your face is just glowing and...I don't know. You seem so happy!"

"That's because I am," she continued with a broad smile. "J.C. and I waited a long, long time for this and I am tired but it doesn't matter. Ma has been good about coming up to help and she sends Esther up every afternoon after school so between the two, I get a little rest. J.C. has been good help, too, more than I would have thought, but then like me, I think he feels blessed more than anything else. And now Fiona is coming, too, J.C.'s mother, so it's all going to work out well."

Jessica thought about how fortunate her friend truly was. She sat back down on the bed momentarily and watched the new mother expertly diaper one baby and then the other before turning back to her.

"Ready for breakfast?"

Becky caught her up as they headed towards the kitchen. "J.C. and Ben are back at work in town. Ma knows you're here so she said she wouldn't be up until later and of course, your brother is down in the camp so it's only you and me."

"I'm not really sure what I'm still doing here, to be honest, or when I'll leave or how. Oh, Becky, it's so much to think about…"

"Jessica, it's not a problem, really. I love having you here. I don't mind you staying longer although I imagine you're anxious to get home. But truly, I hate the idea of seeing you go and I'm not the only one."

"What do you mean?"

Becky dipped a little bacon grease into a skillet from a jar on the back of her gas stove, turned on the burner and cracked two eggs, side by side, once the fat began to sizzle. "I think you know exactly what I mean," Becky added, without looking up from the stove.

"Oh, Becky, don't tease me. Not now." Jessica felt suddenly weary despite the early morning. So many headaches to straighten out. She never imagined life would be more complicated once she left home than it was before. She used to think when she only had to worry about taking care of herself, rather than Grammy, Gabe, Grace and even Jesse, that life would be simpler. How could she have been so mistaken?

"I don't mean to add to your troubles, hon'." Becky reached over and patted Jessica's arm. "I just know that Ben doesn't have any intention of talking about how to get you home on the train or what have you, until after the wedding."

"Wedding? What wedding?"

"Mary Beth Chapman's wedding to a CCC feller this Saturday down at our church."

"Oh my gosh, that's right. She's marrying Spuds Emerson. He was the head cook until he left a week or so ago. He told me he was marrying a girl named Mary Beth from here and he invited me and all his CCC co-workers to the wedding."

"Well, now see, that makes it all real convenient." Becky grinned as she slid the eggs from the skillet onto two plates and added some warm fried bread to each one. "Here." She handed a plate to Jessica and sat down opposite her at the kitchen table.

"Convenient how?"

"Well, 'cause the Chapmans are old family friends of ours, the Darlings, and we're going to the wedding too, and because I think my brother plans on inviting you himself. I do believe he intends to ask you out on a date, my friend."

"Oh, Becky." Jessica eyes rolled towards the ceiling. "What's the point? I mean, it would be lovely, I'm sure, but I've got to go back to Riverton. I don't need any more complications in this whole mess Jesse and I have created."

"A complication? Is that what Ben is now? I think it's a little late for that kind of thinking, don't you?"

Jessica looked down at her plate and wondered how she was going to swallow any of this food with such a lump in her throat. "Oh, I really don't know," she barely breathed. "I don't know but I'm afraid you might be right."

"It's going to be fine, Jessica. I promise. Try to relax and not fret so. Think of it this way. You're going to get a couple of days off, no CCC work, no worrying about hiding out and pretending to be somebody else, no cooking for a bunch of men, no mixing mortar, no hurrying back to Riverton just yet. Just take a couple of days to breathe. I daresay you need it," she added with a soft chuckle.

"I probably do," she admitted as a tear slid down her cheek.

"Well, you don't have to worry about anything, even about my silly brother coming out here and bothering you today. It's Thursday, you know."

"Oh! It is? And he's not coming?"

"Not today. He had to switch days off with someone to get Saturday free to go to the wedding so we'll not see him 'til then. More rest for you. That can't hurt at this point."

"No," Jessica answered wistfully as she began to poke at her egg. "It can't hurt, I guess."

Despite her doubts, the next two days passed

quickly as they melted away into long conversations with Becky and her mother, giggly jokes with Esther, diaper changes, and baby naps. One afternoon, she did slip down the path behind Becky's house to the park below. She walked along the stream, late in the day, deliberately avoiding the presence of any of her former co-workers. She followed the trail down the western side of the spring branch leading from the hatchery to the spring. She stopped once again at the gauge house, hoisted herself into one of the windows overlooking the water and enjoyed a bit of quiet solitude. She was afraid to let her thoughts wander too far afield. She tried hard to follow Becky's advice and not fret too much. Instead, she told herself, simply soak it up and enjoy the beauty that surrounds you, so that when you do leave this place, you will have something special to take with you.

Saturday morning, Ben's car rolled into J.C. and Becky's drive with Jesse in the passenger seat.

"Good morning, boys," Becky called out as she stood at the wash line, hanging out wet clean diapers.

"Hey, Sis," Ben answered back. "Everything going well up here?"

"Fine as frog hair," Becky replied with a grin as she hung up her last diaper.

"Thought we'd come by and say 'hello'," he said as he leaned against the hood of his car.

"Uh-huh." Becky walked towards them.

Jessica came out the front door but stopped on the top stone step of the front porch. "Good morning."

"Good morning," Ben answered. "You look like life out here in the woods is agreeing with you."

"I can't say it isn't," she nodded.

"You got a minute to talk to me?"

"Sure." She stepped off the porch and the two of them strolled up the dirt drive together, back towards the main road.

"I wanted to come see you this morning and ask you something." He hesitated a moment when she remained silent. "I wanted to ask if you would go to Mary Beth Chapman's wedding this afternoon...with me."

She concentrated on the gravel beneath her feet. "I was invited to this wedding a couple of weeks ago by the groom."

"Really?"

"He was my boss in the mess hall when I was cooking in there, Spuds Emerson, but I'd be happy to go with you."

The smile that lit his face stretched from ear to ear. "All right then. I'll...I'll come back." He turned around towards the house to return the way they had come. "I'll be back about...uh, I dunno, this afternoon. The wedding is at 4 pm. You'll be ready, right?"

She laughed at his sudden inability to function. "I'll be ready."

Becky and Jessica combed through Becky's closet as they had a couple of days earlier to find 'real clothes' for her as Jessica called them. This time they looked for a dress for a celebration. "I used to be as little as you…once," Becky laughed, "but it's been a few years. Let's see, if I've still got it. Yes! Here it is." She pulled a pale blue cotton dress, edged in white lace, from the back of her closet. "What do you think?"

It was, without a doubt, the loveliest dress Jessica had ever seen, outside of a magazine. By late afternoon, Becky had helped her to style her quickly returning curls and located a pair of white open-toed shoes that complemented the dress. As they finished preparing, Becky handed Jessica a pair of delicate white cotton gloves. "This will finish your outfit in the latest style," Becky said.

"Oh, they're perfect," Jessica squealed. "Just what I needed too. The camp work certainly has not been kind to my hands. I've used my granny's special hand mix." She drew a small square jar from her bag as she spoke. "But it's nearly all gone now although I've been pretty stingy with it. Kinda had to be careful how and when I put it on. Didn't want to be explaining why a CCC boy smelled of lilacs." She sat the empty jar down on the table.

"Well, I don't know about that, but those are what all the models wear these days in the magazines."

"I love them," Jessica added as she slipped them on. "Thank you so much, Becky. For everything."

"It's the least I can do," Becky laughed. "For the

lady who delivered my babies!"

They giggled happily and Ben found them a few moments later, both dressed and ready for a wedding, while J.C. was still struggling with cuff links and his dress shirt.

"You two go ahead," Becky encouraged as she pushed them towards the front door. "We'll be along shortly after we get the babies loaded into our car."

Outside, Ben took a long step back as they moved towards his vehicle. "Wow. Am I allowed to say that? You look wonderful. You should wear a party dress more often!"

She giggled and blushed at the compliments. "I never thought I would say so but it is nice to wear a dress again. Or at least not be in an old army uniform."

He laughed out loud. "I bet that's true."

"You look awfully nice, not in a uniform, too. Not that you don't look good in that, too. Oh!" She looked down in confusion. "You know what I mean."

"Yes, I think I do."

"The first time I saw you in a deputy's uniform in your pa's barn, I nearly fainted."

"I was that good-looking?" He feigned surprise.

"No, silly." She shook her head. "I was afraid you'd figure me out in short order and take me to jail."

He smiled as he opened the car door for her and

watched her slide into the passenger seat.

At the little white clapboard church down the hill, they found many of their friends gathered outside the church doors and Ben introduced a couple of his to Jessica. Others stood at a distance, however, and simply watched them in silence. They were a handsome couple, Jessica with her dark curls and blue-green eyes and the tall, sandy-haired Ben Darling, who had grown up in this valley. Still, Jessica could not help but fear that many of the stares were all about her change of status. Thankfully, Ben was at her side when she finally caught sight of Percy Lee, John Kelly, and even Captain Smith.

"Come on," Ben said, as she took his arm and they walked in that direction. "Might as well face 'em direct and get it over with, one way or another."

She smiled up at him. She hadn't said a word but still he knew just how she felt.

"Hello," Jessica greeted them shyly. "Percy Lee, how are you? You get all that water coughed up yet?"

"Yeah." He grinned self-consciously and looked sideways at his companions. "Yeah, I did. I'm all right. Thanks to you, they tell me. Guess I'm glad you were there. I don't really remember much of it, in the water, that is. Just remember coughing up water on the rocks and then looking up and seeing you there...Glory Hallelujah, Jess! How'd you do that for so long?"

"Do what?" she asked, watching and trying to

gauge the mood of the others.

"Everything! Girls ain't supposed to be able to work like that and do all the stuff you done, like swim that good. You wouldn't go swimming with us down at the confluence but it wasn't like you couldn't!"

"Uh-huh, and how was I going to go swimming with you boys? In what, my skivvies, like you?"

It was Percy Lee's turn to blush. "Oh, yeah, I didn't think of that."

"Exactly. Believe me. I did. When you invited me to go, I liked to died. I'd have loved to go along but...." She smiled and shrugged.

"But that other stuff, all that mortar-hauling and such?"

"Percy Lee, I didn't do nothing you all weren't doing every day. I was so tired at night I could hardly stand it. You know that but it just had to be done. All of you are here because your family needs you to be. Ain't that the way of it? How many of you would do most anything to make sure the folks back home had enough to eat, a good roof over their head and a safe place to live? I'm no different. My situation was a little more complicated but like you all know now, it was only for a little while. It just had to be done and I was the only one in my family who could do it. I tried to be good. Remember how you all would laugh about me getting out extra early or staying in bed with the covers pulled up over my head? Now you know why! I didn't want to be peeking at your bare backsides. I did my best, fellers, to do what I had to do and to be fair with you. That's all I can say."

She looked down at Becky's delicate little shoes on her feet. She had no intention of coming down here today and making a speech but somehow that is exactly what had happened and now she had no idea how to move on.

She felt Ben's hand drop over hers as it still rested on his arm.

"And you don't have to." Percy Lee stepped forward and held out his hand to her. "You're right, Jess. Jessica? I'll have to get used to that." He shook her hand as if they were meeting for the very first time.

"You can still call me Jess." She smiled up at him. "I don't mind."

"No, no, I can't. 'Cause as I understand it, there's a new Jess here at Bennett Spring. Jess Shine, isn't it? One of those babies you helped with a couple of weeks ago."

Jessica turned to follow his line of sight as Becky, J.C. and their babies came up behind them.

"Well, yes, that's true. His name is Jesse, too, just like my brother. So tell me, how's he doing?" She dropped her voice to a conspiratorial whisper. "You think he's going to make a good CCC man?"

"Oh, yeah." Percy Lee leaned back on his heels and hooked his thumbs in his belt loops. "He'll be all right, after awhile. We'll shape him up pretty quick."

"Oh, good." Jessica laughed easily for the first time since their arrival at the wedding. "You do that. I wouldn't want to leave you short-handed or anything."

"Well, I'm not sure that isn't the case anyway," Captain Smith chimed in. "I mean, can he cook and handle horses and haul mortar as good as you?"

"Oh, I imagine." Jessica laughed again. "He learned it all right there when I did."

Jesse walked up from the far side of the church as she finished. "Learned what?"

She looked him up and down for a long moment before answering. "Life," she answered. "We learned about life." The church doors were opened and the gathered crowd began to file inside.

The church ceremony was short and sweet as a very nervous Stanley "Spuds" Emerson promised to love and cherish his new wife, Mary Beth Chapman. Jessica sat, watching the bride and groom, listening to the preacher as he extolled the virtues of marriage and letting her eyes roam over the assorted guests, from lifelong valley residents to newcomers like herself and her brother. Ben dropped his hand over hers as the preacher finished with the traditional, "You may now kiss your bride, young man."

With that, Spuds' anxiety dissipated suddenly and he gave his new wife an enthusiastic kiss and embrace which the church greeted with light applause and more than a few chuckles.

Outside, as the late afternoon sunshine filtered through the green canopy of elm, hickory and oak trees, the celebration began. A long line of tables held every manner of home-baked and home-canned delicacy, including a lovely three-layered white wedding cake that Mary Beth's Aunt Pearl had carefully constructed over the past twenty-four hours. Smoked ham and fried chicken rounded out the wedding day banquet fit for kings. It was obvious that Mary Beth's family was pulling out all the stops for this party.

"As I understand it, Mary Beth is still miffed with her mother over the dress," Becky whispered to Jessica outside the church.

"Whatever for?" Jessica asked in surprise. "It's a lovely dress."

"Oh, I agree." Becky giggled. "Except that Mary Beth wanted it longer, trailing on the ground like in the storybooks and magazines. Her mother said she wasn't making no dress that was going to get all dirty, dragging all over the ground, so she made it ankle-length instead. I heard Mary Beth was still mad about that!"

"Oh, forevermore!" Jessica shook her head.

"Now her daddy and Spuds put together a wooden dance floor for her," Becky continued, sharing all the local gossip about the wedding. "He said his little girl wants to dance at her wedding and he promised her that she could so he put the dancing floor together in such a way so that afterwards he could take it apart and re-use the wood."

A wooden platform for dancing had been slapped together in the field below the cabins where Jessica had hauled mortar for cabin construction just a few days before, since trusting the soggy ground to be fit for a proper celebration was a risky proposition at best. Fortunately, it had not rained again since the day of the great flood, giving the CCC workers and other valley residents the longest spell of dry weather they had seen all season. Captain Wilbur Smith, amongst others, was hopeful that it was a dry spell that might last awhile.

Some of the boys quickly had a couple of posts driven into the ground at the proper distance and soon the clang of thrown horse shoes could be heard as the men tossed the heavy instruments and hooted and hollered, laughed and teased each other about how close or how far each one landed.

Ben and Jessica found Hannah and Zeb and Esther gathered at a pair of tables and they were joined by Becky, J.C. and their babies.

"So this is the real Jess Newman?" Zeb stood up as they approached and took Jessica's gloved hand in both of his.

"Yes sir," Jessica dropped her eyes to her shoes.

"Well, I have to say, I felt a bit of a fool when I found out about you," Zeb continued, "but then some things made more sense, like the silliness in the air the day I found you and Ben up there at the house in the rain. Other things, like the way you handle those horses, is just downright impressive." He grinned and she felt instantly at ease as she noticed again how much his smile resembled his son's.

A white-haired old man with a polished cedar walking stick slowly approached them, accompanied by Jake Darling, looking the best that Jessica had seen him yet.

"Good evening, ladies and gentlemen," the old man greeted them formally with a broad smile.

"Good evening, Gramps," Zeb answered as he turned and offered the elderly man a place to sit. "Have a seat and rest awhile."

"Don't mind if I do," he returned as he seated himself in slow motion, resting one hand on top of the other, atop his cedar walking stick. "Lovely day for a wedding, don't you know."

"Yes, yes it was," Zeb agreed. "How's life in the hills a-treatin' you these days?"

"Oh fine, fine. Can't complain. Wouldn't sit well with the good Lord if I did," he added with a twinkle in his eye. "I've got a new house guest of late. Have you met?" He nodded his head towards Jake who grinned with his arms folded across his chest.

"I heard something about that," Zeb nodded. "Working out well for you, is it? Or is it more trouble than it's worth?"

"Oh, no, it's been quite a pleasant change," the old man continued. "Haven't had to haul a pail of water now for days. Had more than a couple of hot meals including a very fine passel of fried fish for last night's supper and poke salad to boot. Like I said, can't complain." His smile grew even wider.

Ben stepped up beside his older brother and together, they drifted back a few paces. "How's it going up there at Grampy's place?" Ben asked.

"He's doing all right," Jake nodded, "better than I thought, really. He probably don't eat enough if you ain't watching him but if I make sure the food and water is there handy, he seems to do better with it. I figured with Eldon, Junior and that bunch in jail now, it was safe for us to come out today and join the festivities."

"Well, I'm real glad you did. Guess you heard about us taking those boys in a few days ago?"

"Oh yeah, everybody's talking about it, how the Sheriff dang near shot Junior on his own front porch and you was going to burn down the house to get Eldon out of there," Jake nodded with a smile.

"Well, something like that." Ben laughed as he punched his brother in the arm. "The main thing is we got 'em rounded up and I don't think they'll be bothering anybody for quite some time to come."

"Well, that's the main thing," Jake agreed. "Think I may just stay on awhile up there at Grampy's. We seem to be getting on together just fine and I'm going to cut some wood for him and some others so that'll keep me busy and put a little jingle in our pockets, his wood, my labor."

"That sounds like a good plan for the future, Jake. It really does." Ben smiled as he slid back closer to the rest of the family.

Jesse and Percy Lee stopped to say 'hello' but joined another group of CCC boys who were busy laughing and teasing their erstwhile companion, Spuds. After the food and the cake-cutting, a group of local musicians, mostly members of the Chapman family, gathered at the edge of the dancing platform and began to play. Spuds and Mary Beth broke the ice and stepped onto the platform and danced a slow waltz. Soon others joined them. Jessica hung back, refusing when Ben first asked her to dance.

Percy Lee returned to their table and nervously asked Jessica for a dance. She started to shake her head but she also felt as if everyone's eyes were upon her and she suddenly reversed herself.

Out on the dance floor, she immediately regretted her decision. "I don't dance very well," she muttered as she lightly laid her left hand on Percy Lee's shoulder and allowed him to take her right hand.

"Me, neither," he admitted shyly. "I just wanted a chance to talk to you one more time."

"Percy Lee, you can talk to me any time. That ain't changed."

"Well, yeah it has, Jess. Jessica. You ain't working in the CCC no more and according to what your brother says, you're going back to Riverton here pretty quick. And I just wanted to say…" He took a deep breath. "Well, that one day when we was talking over there under the sycamore tree and I said we was just like brothers. Well, it just ain't so. Even that day, when I thought about it later, you kinda squirmed when I said it—"

"Oh, Percy Lee, I'm so sorry. I felt so guilty, like I was lying to all of you but I didn't know what else to do and—" She looked up at him.

"It's all right, Jessica. Honest. That's what I wanted to tell you. We may not be brothers after all, but I don't mind having me one more sister, if'n it's you."

"Oh, Percy Lee." She leaned her head on his shoulder for the briefest moment. "You have no idea how much I appreciate that."

A tall shadow appeared at her left.

"Hope you don't mind terribly, Percy Lee," Ben spoke up almost apologetically, "but I'd sure like a chance to dance with this lady."

"Oh, I think that could be arranged." Percy Lee's usual near giddy demeanor returned. "She's all yours, Deputy. See ya around, Jessica." He stepped away and to Jessica, in some inexplicable way, it felt as if one door was closing while yet another was opening.

"I don't dance very well," she repeated, to Ben this time.

"Something you don't do well?" He acted surprised as he caught her up in his arms and began to move across the homemade dance floor. "I don't believe it."

"Oh, stop," she responded. "There's lots of things I don't do so well."

"If that be true, all I can say is we haven't seen much of those things since you arrived here at Bennett Spring."

She snorted her response as she tried to watch her feet but found it impossible. "Just stick around awhile, you'll see."

"I'd like to." He dropped his voice to a more serious note. "Actually I'd like you to think about how you might stick around here."

"Nice thought," she replied, "but not too likely. I've got Grammy and Gabe and Grace waiting back home at Riverton. Now that Jesse's here, there ain't an able-bodied person there to help. Grammy can manage for awhile, but she's not getting any younger and it ain't fair to leave her with the care of those two for very long. That same morning that Jesse got hit by that wagon load of logs, she told me how she would like to be out to California with her sister, my great Aunt Hazel. At the time, she laughed and said raising little ones all again had not been in her plans but it was what had to be done at the moment. When she said it, I really didn't understand what she was talking about and why she didn't just take up and go. But now…." A deep sigh escaped her as she frowned. "I guess I can say I really do."

"But what if….?" Ben tried again. "What if….?"

"What if, Ben Darling? For heaven's sakes." Jessica's exasperation threatened to steal the joy of the dance right out from under them. "What if? What if? Why even ask the question when—"

"Hey, calm down, girl. It's just a question, nothing more. Never hurts to ask. Careful now, watch your dancing feet," and with that, he swung her out but the move didn't last long as the musicians changed tempo to another slower song.

Ben pulled her close and hummed along, adding the few words he knew of the Irving Berlin song. "I'll be loving you always," he sang softly, "with a love that's true always."

An overwhelmingly pleasant chill ran up her spine and over her neck and shoulders, making her unsure if she could even keep her feet on the ground, let alone in rhythm to any dance steps. She let her head rest on his shoulder as he continued.

"...not for just an hour, not for just a day, not for just a year, but always."

She savored the moment, reveling in its sweet comfort. Oh, what if indeed!

"You know, I heard that the man who wrote this did it as a wedding gift for his wife. That's pretty incredible, don't you think?"

"Hmmm," she cooed, with her head still on his shoulder. What if, she mused again and then she thought better of it all as she lifted her head suddenly and looked him full in the face.

"Oh, Ben." She broke from his grasp and walked off the dance platform.

"What? What?" He scooted after her and turned her around a few steps away as she headed towards the church and away from the gathered crowd who was obviously going to celebrate well into the night.

"What's wrong? What did I say?"

"It's back to, what if? That's all!" She was practically wailing and she knew it but she couldn't stop herself. "There simply isn't any point, that's all. Can't you see that?"

"No." He managed to get her to stop walking and face him. "No. I can't see that at all. This is what you do when you have a problem. You figure out a way to work it out as my Ma says. You keep thinking about it or as she says, praying about it until you get an answer. You don't just give up!"

"Oh, I can't talk to you about this! You're talking and dreaming about the impossible, that's all. There are three other people caught up in this and I've got to take care of them!"

"Why does it have to be impossible? Three, you say? I thought you said your grandmother wanted to go to California to be with her sister. Then that only leaves two, two little ones at that. That ain't impossible! Don't you see? That's what I think about all the time!"

"What? This? You and me? Staying here?" She threw her hands up in the air and turned away again.

"Yes! You and me and other things, too!"

"Other things? Like what?" she snapped, practically looking for an argument.

"Other things, I dunno. All kinds of things. I think about lots of stuff."

"Name one."

"Okay. The bank robbers."

"The what?"

"The bank robbers. That pair we found up at Junior Kendrix's place. We know they robbed the Rolla bank and we know they came right through here because Cletus Meyers stopped and helped them one night with their car. He was even driving my car when he done it, right here at Bennett Spring, but nobody's ever found the money. Now I think about stuff like that. What if I found that money that Eldon and Herbie stole? It's been driving the sheriff and all them boys crazy. We know they took it and we know they promised some of it to the Kendrix clan for letting 'em stay up there but it wasn't at their place. The sheriff said they were probably afraid to take it up there to Junior's place for fear those boys would take it from them, but I can't help but think, what if I found it? What's wrong with you, Jess? You're looking at me like—"

"What did you say?" Her throat suddenly closed and she could hardly get the words out.

"What do you mean what did I say? I'm trying to give you an answer and explain—"

"What did you say their names were? Herbie? Did you say Herbie?" she croaked again.

"Yeah, I did. Herbie and Eldon. Why?"

"Oh, Ben, come on!" She grabbed his hand and tugged him towards the church.

"What is it?" He scrambled along beside her. "What in the name of all—"

"Shh!" She put a finger to her lips. "Don't say a word! Don't ask a thing. Just come on." She slipped off his sister's high heels and continued barefoot at a clipped pace, carrying the shoes.

He fell in beside her and was amazed how fast she could walk as he found he had to concentrate to keep up. She passed the church and the open field to the left that was to be the site of the new stone dining lodge, the last major construction project in the CCC's building plans for Bennett Spring, according to the plans Captain Smith had shown him one day. They continued on past the road to the right that led up the hill towards Becky and J.C.'s house. Next she marched past the stone-covered double bathroom at the base of the hill.

"Good grief, Jessica!" He could maintain his silence no longer as they approached the hatchery. "Where are we going? Are you going to walk all the way to Bennett Spring itself? It's getting dark, girl, and I don't—"

"Shh!" She shushed him again as she stopped at the triple-arched bridge. "Here." She handed him her shoes and slipped off her gloves and passed them over as well. "Take care of these 'cause they ain't mine and I don't want nothing to happen to them. Stay right here. Don't move. Don't say nothing! Just pray, like your mama says!"

She crossed the bridge as he stood there in the middle of the dirt road. At the far end, she looked first at the small sycamore tree almost in the center of the first section of the bridge and then at the large box elder in the next section and the slender walnut tree at the far eastern end of the bridge, close to the place where she had seen a car hit the bridge nearly two months ago. Cautiously, she stepped around the end of the bridge and disappeared from sight. Ben stood there for several long moments, wondering if the girl of his dreams had lost her mind. He was about to call out despite her warnings when she re-appeared.

"Oh, Ben!" she cried. "Look!" She held a heavy dirt-encrusted canvas bag. "I think this is it!"

"Jessica, how in the world—" he started to ask as she ran awkwardly towards him.

He grabbed her hand and led her over to the soft green grass beneath a sheltering tree, close to the hatchery drive. "What did you find? How did you?" His eyes glowed with surprise and anticipation as he took the sack from her. He beat off some of the dirt to reveal bold black letters. FIRST STATE BANK OF ROLLA.

He opened it and looked inside to discover stacks of bills, bundled together.

"How did you know?"

She smiled broadly at him. "When you said someone helped them in your car and that one of the fellers in the car was named Herbie, that's when I remembered. The first night I snuck out to get a bath in the spring branch..." She hesitated and looked down. "The night Becky told me you found out I wasn't really a CCC boy."

"Yes." He nodded with a wide smile. "I remember that night rather well."

"I'm sure," she muttered. "Well, before I ever got to the water, I saw a car, running without lights and it hit the bridge. Your car came along and of course, at first, I thought it was you. But before your car stopped, the driver of that first car sent the other man to hide under the bridge and he gave him something before he dove under there. At the time, I thought it was all a little strange but I didn't have no idea who they were or why they did that so I just stayed hid and kept real quiet but the one thing I remembered is the driver called the other one Herbie. I never really noticed that after Cletus, is that the name you said? That after Cletus left, the other man came running back to the car and he didn't have that bag no more, but he was all dirty down the front. While he was gone, I heard these strange scraping sounds. It never occurred to me until just now when you were talking up by the dancin' floor what the reason was. Over there, under that big box elder tree, the bottom of it is all surrounded with rocks. Herbie buried that bag under those rocks!"

"Oh, Jessica!" Ben laughed out loud as it all began to make sense.

He dropped the money bag to the ground beneath the tree as he held out his hand to her. "Don't you see? There is no such word as impossible with a girl like you! You just figured out where the bank robbers' loot was and I know, together, we can bring your little brother and sister to this valley, too. Come here." He swung her off of her feet in a half circle and plunked her down lightly to stand in front of him in the moonlight.

She glanced down as she found her footing. "Oh, my stars, Ben! Look at Becky's dress!" she cried out and began to try to beat the dust from the skirt.

"It's all right. Don't worry about it." He laughed and took both of her hands in his. "Right here, right now, Jessica Newman, I'm asking you official. Please, rescue me, like you do everyone you meet. Rescue me, Jessica, right here at Bennett Spring for the rest of my life. Marry me!"

The huge full moon rested in the tops of the trees as if the huge golden orb had been caught in their branches. Pale blue moonlight bathed the entire landscape around them as a soft breeze gently tousled her curls. Jessica contemplated Ben's moonlit figure for a long moment. From the not-so-distant past, Grammy's words echoed back to her. "Your time will come—to go and find your own life. And when it does, you grab it with both hands and hang on tight!"

She tossed Becky's shoes and gloves next to the money sack still on the ground under the tree and threw her arms around his neck.

"Yes, I will," she whispered next to his ear as he hugged her tight. "But only if you promise we'll rescue each other."

The shadow of a great blue heron sailed overhead, above their entwined figures. The blue-green water of the spring branch gurgled beneath the bridge on its way to the Niangua River. Its mighty power as seen in the flood, just a few days earlier, was once again contained. The crystal clear waters of Bennett Spring had returned to their usual role of blessing the days of residents and visitors alike with their serene beauty. And as always, the heart of the spring lives on, bringing life and a promising future to the next generation.

HISTORICALLY SPEAKING...

- The Civilian Conservation Corps (CCC) worked at Bennett Spring State Park for four years from 1933 through 1937. The 1772nd Company Sp-Mo-7 was organized at Ft. Leavenworth, Kansas and actually consisted of 198 World War I veterans, ten of whom worked the entire span of time the CCC was located at Bennett Spring. Over the course of the years at Bennett Spring, 925 men served in that company. Their work at Bennett Spring included: the construction of a dam that replaced the original crib dam, the well-known triple-arched bridge, the dining lodge, the store and post office building (located approximately on the site of the current hatchery garage building and demolished in 1982 when the new store was completed), the picnic shelter house near the spring, the nearby gauge house on the spring branch bank, roads and trails and six individual cabins, located along the base of the hillside behind the park pool. Two of those were also demolished and replaced by the current multiplex cabins, built in the early 1980s; one burned accidentally and three have been completely renovated in the ensuing years with modern appliances and continue in use. The current park office and some of the shop buildings were also built by the CCC during their stay at Bennett Spring.

• The CCC at Bennett Spring also dismantled all but the last of the buildings of the village of Brice, Missouri during the 1930s. They renovated the mill which continued in use in one form or another, including grinding fish feed in its later years, until it burned in 1944. The old hotel was also dismantled in that same year. The Bennett Spring Church of God, once a white clapboard building, was covered in stone to more closely match other park buildings in 1954, per current members of the church, long after the CCC was gone. It is the only building of Brice that still exists. Since it is within the confines of a state park, the one acre plot on which the church stands is independent of the park, exempted from state ownership by the original contract that was made with the Bennett family in 1924. Likewise, the large cedar tree outside the Bennett Spring Park Store in the 21st century stood in what was then an open field between the town of Brice and the Bennett Spring Mill in 1935.

- The spring and early summer of 1935 was one of the wettest seasons on record and did greatly inhibit the work of the CCC workers in the park at that time. The flood of June 1935 damaged park grounds, including many of the newly-completed projects such as trails, roads and hatchery improvements. The CCC project superintendent at the time also made complaints to his superiors that he did not have enough trucks to complete the work at hand.

- The first buildings the CCC workers completed at Bennett Spring were their own barracks, all of which they dismantled before leaving, with one exception. The officers' barracks building located on the hillside behind the current hatchery garage and mentioned in this story as the location of the captain's office still stands although it has been abandoned for more than two decades. Over the years, it has served as a hotel and a barracks building for Missouri state honor farm prisoners who worked at the park on a regular basis during the 1970s. It is one of only two CCC barracks buildings still standing in the state. The stone foundation work of another CCC building remains, close along the hillside behind the CCC rest room building, northwest of the current hatchery garage building, and is believed to have been used as a hospital by the CCC workers.

- According to Bob Dampier, a Bennett Spring area native, the park's famous triple-arched bridge was actually built by a Kansas City construction firm that brought cranes and other equipment to the park area at the time. His uncle, Lonnie Davison and his aunt, Mae Olden were both employees of the L.G. Barcus Construction Company of Kansas City and met on the Bennett Spring job. The family has several affidavits regarding the construction and has tried unsuccessfully to ascertain appropriate recognition from the state of Missouri. According to their information, one of the construction stone masons is also the person who trained several CCC workers on the proper way to cut and apply the stone veneer over the concrete structure we all love today as the Bennett Spring Bridge. The Bennett Spring Bridge and several other buildings in the park are listed on the National Register of Historic Places.

- The gauge house or recorder house was one of the earliest structures completed by the CCC at Bennett Spring. While some equipment set up in the little building back in the 1930s may account for its original design, that information has been lost to time. In more recent years, a measuring stick device was installed by the US Geological Survey (USGS) to read the amount of water supplied by Bennett Spring which is approximately 100,000,000 gallons daily. For many years, park personnel read that measuring stick device on a daily basis. The USGS eventually replaced the stick device with a float system device that took measurements hourly and included the use of the brown metal box that still sits in the gauge house window. In 2007, the USGS installed the current computerized recording device which includes a solar panel and an antenna, takes measurements every 15 minutes and is located just outside the picturesque historic stone building known as the gauge house.

- Pictures, tools, other items and more information about the CCC and their accomplishments at Bennett Spring State Park can be found and enjoyed by the public at the displays at the Bennett Spring Nature Interpretive Center.

A BRIEF HISTORY

The first visitors to what we now call Bennett Spring were barefoot and later moccasin-footed. Members of the Osage, the Delaware and Kickapoo tribes were known to have hunted, fished and camped in the area. There is some conviction amongst early historians that the People of the Middle Waters, as the Osage called themselves, did not actually live at or around the spring, but rather simply passed through, believing this to be a sacred area, a place they held in high respect.

They shared a legend that described the original site of the spring as a small pool of great depth. Their best divers could not reach the bottom, despite its calm waters which produced only a small stream of water. Their stories relate that those original native people forgot their traditions, who they were and where they came from. They became proud and arrogant, forgetting their daily prayers and neglecting their responsibilities as stewards of the land that had been entrusted to them by the Sacred One. They killed other Indians and took the scalps of those who were not worthy. One night, after they had returned from yet another shameful raid, the Sacred One's wrath was felt by all as the ground shook, nearby trees tumbled and the earth as they knew it changed forever. The quiet pool became a boiling spring, as ceaseless tears began to flow from the eye of the Sacred One, creating a full and flowing stream that followed along the valley floor all the way to the Niangua River over a mile away. Bennett Spring, the spring we know that produces 100 million gallons of cool fresh water daily, was born.

By the early 1800s, the Osage, the primary Indian tribe of this area, left of their own accord as their chief, Pawhuska, moved his people to lands in Kansas. Many years later, the Osage moved on to what is today still Osage County in Oklahoma. By the 1830s, the U.S. Army made certain that all other Indians had been pushed westward, leaving behind only thousands of arrowheads, souvenirs that today decorate the mantels of many local residences and on rare occasion, still delight a sharp-eyed tourist.

In 1837 James Brice, originally from Virginia, and his wife, Ann, of Kentucky, arrived in the valley from Illinois. The forest of oak, hickory, black walnut, elm, maple and dogwood grew dense with underbrush and bears, wolves, panthers, wildcats and even the occasional buffalo were also common. Smaller animals such as raccoons, rabbits, squirrels, deer, fox, beaver, mink, muskrat and wild turkey, most of which can still be seen on occasion, abounded.

In the early 1840s James Brice, then 50 years old, built the first of several mills in the Bennett Spring area. As other settlers moved into the valley the area became known as Brice Spring. The small village that sprang up on the site of today's Bennett Spring State Park Store was later called Brice, Missouri beginning in the 1860s after the death of James Brice.

Within a few years other settlers and families moved into the valley—Hawk, Brown, Conn, Clanton, Henson, Lomax, Mullicaine and Bennett. Peter M. Bennett constructed a second mill at the confluence, where the spring waters meet the Niangua River, but within a few short years, both mills were destroyed by flood waters.

James Brice's daughters, Jane and Anna, grew up and married others in the valley; Jane to Asahel Bennett and Anna, per her father's wishes, married John Clanton, a young wagon maker from North Carolina. He and Anna had two children, Nancy Jane and James Madison Clanton, before John Clanton's death in the winter of 1856 at the age of 30. Shortly afterwards in early 1857, Anna Brice Clanton gave birth to her third child, Anna Caroline.

By the 1860s the country as a whole was engaged in the Civil War but the spring area and the tiny town of Brice were protected by their secluded location and lack of a nearby railhead.

The widow Anna Brice Clanton remarried, to Peter M. Bennett Jr. this time. The 427 acres of property, including the spring itself that had once belonged to her father and had been willed by him to her first husband, John Clanton, now reverted fully to her. Upon her marriage to Peter Bennett Jr., all of her property became his and soon the general area became known as Bennett Spring. Peter and Anna Bennett had six children but only two lived to adulthood, William Sherman and Josephine Bennett.

In 1894 the Rev. George Bolds, his wife, Mary, and their four children, the oldest being a 17-year old daughter, Louie Bolds, came to Bennett Spring and held the first of many old time revivals. At their first meeting, 38 men and women were saved and baptized including 29 year old William Sherman Bennett. A year later, he and Louie Bolds were married. In the years to come, Louie and later her son, Paul, would become well known ministers throughout the area.

The record is vague as to exactly how many mills were eventually built in the valley. The two original grain mills were both known to have been destroyed by flood and the last mill built by Peter Bennett was constructed close to the village of Brice. It burned in 1895. The last Bennett Spring mill, a grist mill, stood near the location of the previous mill, across the section of land that today holds the concrete hatchery pools built in the 1960s. This mill was a partnership amongst J.H. Hensley, a local cattleman, and Dr. John B. Atchley, Arminta

Atchley, John B.'s wife and J. H. Hensley's sister, and Freeman Atchley, a brother-in-law to Hensley and Arminta Atchley.

The new mill partners took out a ninety-nine year lease with W.S. and Louie Bennett for use of the wheel left from the 1895 mill that had burned, the dam floor, water and roadway use rights necessary for the operation of the mill.

The new mill, opened in 1900, once again drew people to Bennett Spring to fish and camp while they waited in line for their wheat to be ground. Meanwhile, a report in the *Laclede County Sentinel* in January 1900 stated that the Missouri Fish Commissioner deposited 40,000 mountain trout into the spring branch, brought from west of the Continental Divide. While several others, visitors and residents alike, expressed an interest in stocking more trout in the area, an Oklahoma dentist, Charles A. Furrow, and an unnamed business partner were the first to actually invest in the idea by establishing a hatchery at Bennett Spring in July 1923.

Others began to come to Bennett Spring driving Model A's and Model T's or a rented buggy from Lebanon to picnic, visit or even spend a night or two at the Brice Inn, run by Josephine "Josie" Bennett. The residents of the village of Brice, never prosperous by any stretch of the imagination, continued in their daily lives and welcomed the growing number of visitors to their valley.

According to an article that appeared in the December 12, 1924 issue of the *Laclede County Republican*, A.O. Mayfield, the president of the

Lebanon Chamber of Commerce, requested that state officials consider Laclede County as a possible site for the first state park.

Soon after negotiations began however, they were publicly called off as the parties involved could not agree. They began again shortly afterwards and on December 27, 1924, Josie Bennett Smith sold the state their first acquisition of land, 8.5 acres for the new Bennett Spring State Park.

In April 1925, William Sherman Bennett sold 565 acres of land to the state that would become the heart of Bennett Spring State Park and 427 of those acres could be traced directly to his grandfather, James Brice, the original settler at Bennett Spring.

The state gave full power and authority over the new lands to the Lebanon Chamber of Commerce to collect and receive rents on current leases until the state could take proper control of its new property. Arlie Bramwell, a great-great-grandson of James Brice, was hired as the first superintendent of both the park and the hatchery. Life in Brice, Missouri continued basically uninterrupted for a few more years, despite the change of ownership of the land.

The Great Depression changed many things in America and by 1933, one in four persons throughout the U.S. had lost their job, their home or both. The Civilian Conservation Corps, one of several Federal programs designed to put people back to work and put the country back on sound economic footing, provided hundreds of workers with desperately needed work with many different projects and Bennett Spring Park was one of them.

The CCC work at Bennett Spring is well-known and well-documented. In 1938, the year after the CCC left the area, records indicate 53,762 persons visited Bennett Spring, ten percent of the total visitors that year to Missouri's twenty-five state parks. Bennett Spring State Park was then and continues to be a well-established jewel of the Missouri State Park system.

OTHERS BOOKS
BY LAURA L. VALENTI

Novels

The Heart of the Spring
The Heart of the Spring Comes Home
The Heart of the Spring Everlasting

*

Between the Star and the Cross: The Choice
Between the Star and the Cross: The Election
Between the Star and the Cross: The Promise

*

Las Palomitas: The Little Doves
A Story of El Salvador

*

Non-Fiction

Ozark Meth: A Journey of Destruction and
Deliverance
By Dick Dixon and Laura L. Valenti